"You Have Tw[o] Glendovia, And [I'll] Enjoy Them. To Enjoy You."

Nicolas moved closer, his arms drawing her into his embrace. "I know that you'll need to spend your days working. But your evenings will be free. And I'll expect you to spend them with me, in my bed."

"Absolutely not." Alandra shook her head and took a step back, breaking away from his touch.

As much as he wanted to close the distance between them and kiss the quarrel from her lips, he remained where he was, allowing her to believe a few inches of space would keep her safe from him.

Dear Reader,

I've always wanted to write a story involving some type of royalty…a prince hero or princess heroine. I also knew that I wanted to give Alandra Sanchez, whom I introduced in my February 2007 Silhouette Desire book, *Blackmailed into Bed,* a very special hero of her own. Well, what could be more special than a prince, right? Putting them both together seemed like the perfect solution. Add to that the opportunity I was given to set this story during the holidays, and I was one happy camper!

I hope you enjoy *Christmas in His Royal Bed* and this little jaunt through the island kingdom of Glendovia.

And don't forget to visit my Web site, www.HeidiBetts.com, as often as you like for information about all of my books!

Happy holidays!

Heidi Betts

HEIDI BETTS

CHRISTMAS IN HIS ROYAL BED

Silhouette® Desire

Published by Silhouette Books
America's Publisher of Contemporary Romance

SILHOUETTE BOOKS

ISBN-13: 978-0-373-76833-2
ISBN-10:   0-373-76833-8

CHRISTMAS IN HIS ROYAL BED

Visit Silhouette Books at www.eHarlequin.com

Printed in U.S.A.

Books by Heidi Betts

Silhouette Desire

Bought by a Millionaire #1638
Blame It on the Blackout #1662
When the Lights Go Down #1686
Seven-Year Seduction #1709
Mr. and Mistress #1723
Bedded Then *Wed* #1761
Blackmailed into Bed #1779
Fortune's Forbidden Woman #1801
Christmas in His Royal Bed #1833

HEIDI BETTS

An avid romance reader since junior high school, Heidi knew early on that she wanted to write these wonderful stories of love and adventure. It wasn't until her freshman year of college, however, when she spent the entire night reading a romance novel instead of studying for finals, that she decided to take the road less traveled and follow her dream. As well as devoting her time to reading, writing and creating romance, she is the founder of her local Romance Writers of America chapter. She also has a tendency to take injured and homeless animals of every species into her Central Pennsylvania home.

Heidi loves to hear from readers. You can write to her at P.O. Box 99, Kylertown, PA 16847 (a SASE is appreciated, but not necessary) or e-mail heidi@heidibetts.com. And be sure to visit www.heidibetts.com for news and information about upcoming books.

In loving memory of Helen Brown. When she passed away this time last year after a long and valiant battle with breast cancer, I lost a friend, and the romance world lost a dedicated fan. We miss you, Helen. And if Heaven is any kind of Heaven at all, it will be filled with romance novels for you to enjoy.

And with much appreciation to loyal reader Jennifer Yates, who, when I challenged readers to help me out, came up with many of the names used in this story. Thanks, Jennifer!

One

*O*nly she would do.

Prince Stephan Nicolas Braedon of Glendovia watched the ebony-haired beauty from afar. Tall and lithe, with an hourglass figure, she had silky black hair that fell in a straight curtain to her hips. He was too far away to know the color of her eyes or see the full pout of her lips, but he trusted the feeling in his gut that told him both would be just as alluring as the rest of her.

Cocking his head toward the tall, suited man

at his side, he said in a low voice, "Find out her name."

His bodyguard followed the direction of his gaze, then gave a stiff nod before moving away. Nicolas didn't need to ask how Osric intended to get the information, nor did he care.

A few minutes later, his bodyguard returned, standing at attention at Nicolas's side.

"Her name is Alandra Sanchez, Your Highness. She is in charge of the organization of this evening's event."

Alandra. A beautiful name for a beautiful woman.

She floated around the large, crowded ballroom, smiling, chatting with guests, making sure everything was running smoothly. The full-length lavender gown she wore shimmered in the muted lighting every time she moved, and fit her perfect feminine curves like a glove.

Nicolas hadn't attended this fund-raising dinner in hopes of finding a lover, but now that he'd seen her, he knew he wouldn't be leaving the United States without making arrangements for her to become his next mistress.

It was true that he was the member of the royal

family in charge of overseeing Glendovia's charitable organizations, but his duties did not extend to attending charitable events outside of his own country. That, he usually left to his sister or one of his two brothers.

But though his sister, Mia, had been scheduled to make the trip to the States and attend this dinner to raise funds for a new children's wing at a central Texas hospital, she'd had to cancel at the last minute. Since Nicolas was to meet with very wealthy oilmen to discuss fuel for his country, he decided to attend.

Until a few minutes ago, he had been resenting the interruption of his own life and plans, and all but cursing his sister for being the cause. Now, however, he was considering sending Mia a bouquet of flowers or a box of her favorite truffles. He wanted to thank her for putting him on a path to what could turn out to be an extremely pleasurable experience.

Smiling so brightly the muscles in her cheeks ached, Alandra Sanchez moved around the room, making sure everything was running smoothly. She'd been working to set up this gala for months now, in hopes of raising both awareness and money for the new children's hospital wing.

Unfortunately, things weren't going quite as well as she'd hoped, and Alandra knew she had only herself to blame.

Everyone in the room seemed to be watching her. She could see their curiosity. Sense their condemnation.

All because she'd had the dreadful misfortune to get mixed up with the wrong man.

Of all the things that could have happened to put a damper on this evening's event, this was the worst. A hurricane, a flash flood, even the hotel catching on fire…

Those were all disasters she could have handled. They barely would have caused a blip on her radar. But instead, she was being personally attacked, her reputation besmirched.

It served her right for ever getting involved with Blake Winters in the first place. She should have known the minute she met him that he would end up causing her nothing but trouble.

And now everyone in this room—everyone in Gabriel's Crossing, the great state of Texas and

possibly the entire United States of America—
thought she was a home-wrecking adulteress.

That's what the newspaper gossip columns
were saying about her. Her picture, along with
Blake's and that of his wife and two children, had
been plastered everywhere, with glaring, slander-
ous headlines.

Ignoring the stares and whispers she knew were
aimed in her direction, Alandra held her head high
and continued wending her way through the ballroom, acting as though nothing was wrong. As
though her heart wasn't racing, her face wasn't
flushed with humiliation and her palms weren't
damp with anxiety.

Nothing that had happened in the week since
the story of her affair with Blake Winters broke had
led her to believe the fund-raising dinner wouldn't
still be a complete success. None of the invited
guests had cancelled, making excuses for why they
couldn't attend. No one from the hospital benevo-
lence society had called to complain about the
scandal she found herself suddenly embroiled in,
or to voice concerns about her name being linked
to the organization.

All of which led her to believe everything would be fine. That even though reporters were camped out on her front lawn, the rest of her life continued to run smoothly.

Now, though, she wasn't so sure. Now, she thought perhaps every seat in the room was filled because the cream of central Texas high society wanted an up-close-and-personal glimpse of one of their own who had so recently fallen from grace.

She might as well have a scarlet letter pinned to her chest or a piece of spinach stuck in her teeth, for all the attention being focused on her every move.

The attention—even negative attention—she could handle. What concerned her more than the stares and whispers was the impact her newly sullied reputation might have on the amount of money collected this evening.

She'd worked so hard to put this event together, was so passionate about her philanthropy, giving of both her time and money to support the causes she felt most strongly about. And she had always been quite successful in convincing others to give to those causes, too.

Usually, by this point in the evening, she would

already have collected a dozen extremely generous checks slipped to her by those in attendance,
with more to follow at the end of the night. Tonight, however, her hands—and the hospital's cof-
fers—were still empty.

Because she'd had the misfortune of meeting
Blake Winters at another fund-raiser last year, and
hadn't been wise enough to turn him away when
he'd started asking her out, those who were most
in need could very well end up going without.

The prospect broke her heart, and she pressed
a hand to the snug satin stays sewn into the lining
of her gown in an attempt to settle the nervous cat-
erpillars squirming and wiggling in her belly.

She would act as though nothing was wrong,
nothing was out of the ordinary—and pray like
the dickens that the crowd got over their curiosity and remembered their true purpose for
being here before the evening was over. Otherwise, she had a sneaking suspicion her personal
bank account would be taking a hard hit when
she attempted to single-handedly make up for
what the children's wing fund should have
earned tonight. And probably would have, if not

for her bad luck and some of the poor decisions she'd made recently.

Once she'd made her loop through the crowd to be sure every seat was filled, every guest served and everything was running as smoothly as possible, she returned to her own place at the front of the room, where a raised dais had been set up for the event's organizers. She made small talk with the women on either side of her and choked down her meal, barely tasting a bite.

Next came a speech from the organization's president, and a short ceremony where plaques were given to several members who had gone above and beyond in the past year. Even Alandra received one, for her continued dedication to raising money for the hospital.

Finally, the evening drew to an end, and she breathed a sigh of relief. She was now holding a few generous checks, and had received promises for more. Not as many as she'd collected in the past, and she had definitely noticed a distinct difference in the way people had treated her throughout the evening. But at least things were looking a bit brighter than they had when the night began.

She made a final round of the room, nodding farewells to guests as they exited the ballroom, and making sure no one left anything behind before the hotel staff started cleaning up.

Gathering her own small, beaded clutch and shawl from her seat, she found her mind racing ahead to what she needed to do the next day—thoughts that were interrupted when she heard a low, masculine voice call her name.

"Miss Sanchez?"

Turning, she found herself dwarfed by a wide-shouldered, dark-haired mountain of a man.

She swallowed once before pasting a smile on her face and tipping her head up, up, up to meet his gaze.

"Yes?"

"If you have a minute, my employer would like to speak with you."

He inclined his head, drawing her attention to the back of the room, where a lone gentleman sat at one of the now-cleared round tables.

From what she could see at this distance, he was quite handsome.

He was also staring at her.

"Your employer?" she asked.

"Yes, miss."

So much for gaining more information about who, exactly, the mountain's employer was.

But if he had attended tonight's dinner, then he was likely a current or potential donor, and she always had time to speak with a contributor. Especially one who could afford his own bodyguard, or CIA agent, or professional wrestler....

"Of course," she said, maintaining her bright, upbeat demeanor.

Turning sideways, the giant gestured for her to move ahead of him, and then escorted her across the nearly empty room. Around them, dishes clinked and stacked chairs clattered as the kitchen and cleaning staff worked to disassemble what had taken all day to set up.

As she approached the man who wished to speak with her, he lifted a flute of champagne and took a long sip.

He wore a smartly tailored jacket of navy blue, cut quite differently than most of those she'd seen throughout the night. He definitely was not a local.

She also noticed that her earlier perception of

him being "quite handsome" was a gross inaccuracy. He was movie-star gorgeous, with dark hair and startling blue eyes that seemed to bore into her like laser beams.

Holding out her hand, she introduced herself. "Hello, I'm Alandra Sanchez."

"I know," he replied, taking her hand and refusing to let it go as he tugged her gently forward. "Have a seat, won't you, please."

Letting her shawl fall lower on her bare back, she slid onto the chair beside him. "Your…employee said you wanted to speak to me."

"Yes," he replied slowly. "May I offer you a glass of champagne?"

She opened her mouth to refuse, but the hulk was already pouring and setting a glass in front of her.

"Thank you."

Though they both had drinks now, and the evening's event was clearly over, the man seated beside her still didn't speak. The silence made Alandra shift uncomfortably, and caused gooseflesh to break out along her arms.

"What did you need to speak with me about,

Mr...." she finally pressed, careful to remain as polite as possible.

"You may call me Nicolas," he replied.

His voice carried a slight accent. Perhaps the hint of a British lilt, but Alandra couldn't place it.

"Nicolas," she repeated, because he seemed to expect it. Then she continued in her attempts to get to his reason for wanting to speak with her.

"Were you interested in making a donation to the fund for the new children's cancer wing of the hospital?" she asked. "If so, I would be happy to accept a check tonight. Or if you'd prefer, I can put you in touch with someone from the organization you can speak with, to make your contribution personally."

For a moment after she finished, he simply continued to study her, his lapis-blue eyes sharp and commandingly intense.

After taking another sip of the expensive champagne, he slowly said, "I would be happy to give to your little…cause. However, that is not why I invited you over here."

Alandra's eyes widened fractionally at that, but she did her best to hide her consternation.

"I am staying in a suite of rooms here in this hotel," he informed her. "I'd like for you to return there with me. Spend the rest of the evening in my bed. If things go well and we are…compatible, perhaps we can discuss further arrangements."

Alandra blinked, but otherwise remained frozen in place, her entire body mannequin-stiff and un-moving. She couldn't have been more stunned if he'd lifted a hand and slapped her across the face.

She didn't know what to say. Didn't know what she *should* say.

This certainly wasn't the first time she'd been propositioned. Young or old, rich or poor, men had always been attracted to her, and she'd had more than her share of invitations to dinner, the theater, even romantic jaunts to private island hideaways.

And, yes, she was well aware that every single one of those men had hopes that dinner, the the-ater and tropical getaways would help him to se-duce her into his bed.

But never—*never*—had any of them been so bold, so brash, as to flat-out ask her to sleep with him.

This was all because of the scandal, she realized

suddenly, her spine snapping straight with offense. Those bloody articles had labeled her an immoral home wrecker. And this man had obviously gotten wind of that and decided she wouldn't be averse to an indecent proposal.

Well, she was averse. She was disgusted and thoroughly insulted.

Pushing her chair back, she rose to her feet, rearranged her shawl across her back and arms, and tightened her fingers on her small clutch purse. Concentrating on her breathing, she stood perfectly rigid, looking down at him.

"I don't know what kind of woman you think I am. But I can assure you I'm *not* the kind to go to bed with a man I've just met."

She cut a quick glance at the bear standing at attention a yard or two away. "Maybe your bodyguard can find someone a little more willing and a lot less discriminating to go back to your room with you tonight. That is, if you're utterly incapable of finding her on your own."

With that, Alandra turned on her heel and marched out of the ballroom to the elevator.

Just who the hell did the man think he was?

Two

Who did she think she was to speak to him in such a manner?

Nicolas had never been turned down like that before.

He blinked once, slowly, searching his memory for a similar incident that might have taken place during his lifetime.

No, he didn't think he'd been turned down *ever*.

Had she actually implied that he was incapable of finding his own female companionship? Or that he had to order Osric to *pay* a woman to spend time with him?

He shook his head, still not quite believing what had just taken place. Behind him, Osric shuffled closer, looming over his right shoulder.

"Your Highness, shall I go after her and bring her back so that you may finish your conversation?"

Nicolas could picture his oversize bodyguard, who closely resembled a brick wall, tackling Miss Sanchez to the ground and carting her back to him…and the fuss the lady would kick up if he so much as tried.

"No, thank you, Osric," he replied. "I believe I'll be returning to the suite alone this evening."

Placing his hands on the tabletop in front of him, he stood and straightened the front of his jacket, then started out of the ballroom, with his trusty security guard close on his heels.

He should be upset, Nicolas thought, as they made their way through the hotel to his private, luxurious suite on the thirty-third floor.

Ironically, he was more intrigued than ever by the ebony-haired beauty. It was her face and figure that had first caught his attention, and seeing her up close hadn't changed his mind about having her in his bed.

He would have expected a dressing-down such as she'd given him to turn him off, to make him realize he didn't want to sleep with a woman who possessed such a sharp tongue. Instead, her spirit fired his blood.

If anything, he found himself wanting her more. She was lovely and fierce, and he could only imagine how passionately those qualities would translate between the sheets.

Alandra Sanchez might think she'd gotten in the last word downstairs, when she'd all but told him to take his offer and go straight to the devil. But Prince Stephan Nicolas Braedon was used to getting his way, getting what he wanted.

And he wanted *her.*

So he would have her. He only had to figure out how.

One week later…

"Pop? Alandra? Is anybody here?"

Alandra heard her sister calling from downstairs,

and was more than happy to take a break from the event plans she'd been working on all afternoon.

Since Elena had moved out of their father's house and into her own with her new husband, Chase, Alandra didn't get to see her as often as she used to.

Abandoning her desk, she found her sister looking slightly frazzled as she flipped through a pile of mail stacked beside a large arrangement of fresh flowers on the round table in the center of the foyer. When she heard Alandra's approach, Elena raised her head and rolled her eyes.

"A reporter tried to follow my car through the security gate," she snapped, waving a hand over her shoulder in the direction of the front door. "He was camped out front, waiting."

Alandra frowned, moving closer to give her sister a gentle squeeze. "I'm so sorry. I really thought they'd have lost interest by now and moved on to something else."

"It's not your fault," Elena said with a sigh, returning Alandra's hug. "And eventually they *will* lose interest and move on."

"So what are you doing here?" she asked distractedly, her mind still on the reporter. It was one thing for *her* to be harassed and annoyed because of her own foolish actions, but it was another for her family to be dragged into this mess.

"Since Chase won't be home for dinner because of a late meeting, I thought I'd stop by to say hello, see how you and Pop are doing, and grab a bite to eat. Not to mention picking up any stray mail," she added, stuffing a few letters into the side pocket of her handbag.

Her sister had married and moved out last year, but the change-of-address process took time, and the odd letter or piece of mail showed up for her occasionally.

"Well, dinner will be served at seven, as usual, and as far as I know, everything is fine around here. Pop is still at the office, and I've just been working on the plans for that fund-raiser for the animal shelters."

"Will Chase and I be invited?" Elena asked.

"Of course."

"Looks like you got something important," her sister said, nodding toward the letter left on top of the stack.

Alandra picked up the thick envelope and read the return address, which was embossed in dark blue, fancy raised script on parchment-quality stationery. "H.R.H. Prince Stephan Nicolas Braedon, Kingdom of Glendovia."

"His Royal Highness?" Elena asked. "Really? You got a letter from a prince?"

"It appears so." She opened the envelope and skimmed the official-looking letterhead and neatly typed text of the top page. Then, heart stuttering, she read it again. "Oh, my God," she breathed.

"What?"

"This Prince Stephan wants me to come to his kingdom and oversee all of their fund-raising organizations."

Both sisters scanned the letter. It touched on Alandra's past fund-raising accomplishments, which the prince claimed were very impressive, and stressed how much Glendovia could use her assistance. He even went so far as to enclose copies of a contract for her employment that he hoped she would peruse and strongly consider signing.

Lifting the cover sheet, Alandra read the one-page agreement. It briefly outlined her duties and obligations, if she chose to accept the royal family's offer, as well as their obligations to her.

"Do you think this is legitimate?" Elena demanded.

The Braedon name did ring some bells. "I guess it would be easy enough to check out," she replied.

The two of them went into Alandra's office, where she started going through her guest lists, and her sister did a quick search on the Internet.

"Huh," Elena said when they discovered at almost the same moment that Stephan Nicolas Braedon was, indeed, a bona fide prince, and the island of Glendovia really did exist. According to Alandra's records, another member of the Braedon royal family—a Princess Mia—had attended one of her recent fund-raisers.

"What are you going to do?" Elena asked.

"Well, I'll reply, of course, and thank him for the generous offer, but I can't possibly accept. I'm already knee-deep in organizing my next event, and Christmas is a month off. I don't want to be away from my family over the holidays."

"I don't blame you, but you have to admit it's a flattering offer."

Extremely flattering, Alandra thought, glancing once again at the raised script of the letterhead. She almost wanted to reach out and run her fingertips over the prince's name. Her letter of refusal definitely wouldn't be an easy one to write.

"But maybe…"

Alandra glanced at her sister. "What?"

"I was just thinking that maybe this position in Glendovia is exactly what you need."

Alandra frowned. "What?"

"Well, things are anything but simple around here for you right now. You've got a reporter camped outside the house, that jerk Winters still calling you, and…well…" Her gaze skittered away and her voice softened slightly. "I heard that last week's fund-raiser didn't go as well as your events usually do."

Alandra took a breath, trying not to let the pain of having her shortcomings pointed out by her own flesh and blood overwhelm her.

Running a supportive hand down her arm, Elena continued. "I was just thinking that if you got away for a while, where no one could find you, this would all blow over. And when you came back, you could get on with your life as though none of it had ever happened."

"But I would be away from you guys," Alandra murmured. "Over Christmas."

"You could come back before then. But even if you didn't, it's only one holiday. There's always next year." Wrapping an arm around her shoulders, her sister added, "I don't necessarily *want* you to go, I'm just saying that maybe you should think it over and do what's best for you. I think Pop would agree."

"I'll consider it," Alandra said, realizing her sister was making a good point. Perhaps the best way to leave all this scandal behind *was* to fly off to a foreign country.

Three

Less than a week later, the Saturday after Thanksgiving, Alandra arrived on the island of Glendovia, hoping against hope that she'd made the right decision.

Her flight had been uneventful. And a limousine had been waiting at the airport for her, as promised in the itinerary that had been faxed to her as soon as she'd accepted Prince Stephan's offer.

Staring out the window as the car sped through the countryside, Alandra was swept away by the beauty of the tiny island country. Located in a northern area of the Mediterranean, it was postcard perfect, with a clear azure sky, rolling emerald hills, and the sprawling blue-green of the sea visible in the distance.

Even what she assumed to be the center of the capital seemed more quaint and clean than anywhere she'd traveled in America or Europe. The buildings were tall, but not mammoth. The streets were busy, but not crowded and harried.

Things seemed more tranquil here, and for the first time since scrawling her name across the bottom of that employment contract, she thought she might actually be glad she'd agreed to come.

Her family had supported the decision wholeheartedly, wanting her to be happy and get away from the scandal they knew was causing her such pain. She had accepted the position in order to protect them from a part of her life that had gotten ugly, in hope it would not spill over onto them.

The limousine slowed and waited for a tall, antique iron gate to slide open. They drove up a long, winding lane that ran among pristine, well-manicured lawns and gardens.

The house—*palace* was a better word—was somewhat historical in design, but looked updated and modern. Eggshell-white, with pillars and balconies and a myriad of floor-to-ceiling windows, it stood atop a small rise overlooking the splashing waves of the Mediterranean.

As the driver opened the door and helped her out of the vehicle, she couldn't tear her eyes away from the breathtaking view. Alandra continued to gawk while the driver removed her bags from the trunk and escorted her to the front door.

A butler opened it and invited her inside, where a handful of maids dressed in matching gray uniforms collected her luggage and trotted off with it.

The butler said, "The prince has requested you be brought to him immediately upon your arrival, Miss Sanchez. If you'll follow me."

Feeling as though she'd just stepped into a fairy tale, Alandra did just that, taking in every detail of the foyer as they passed.

The floor was of highly polished marble in squares of black and a mottled gray-white. A chandelier the size of a small bus hung overhead, with thousands of dangling crystals twinkling in the natural light. Directly across from the front entrance stood a wide staircase leading halfway to the second level before branching off to either side.

The butler led her to the right of the foyer and down a carpeted corridor lined with priceless artwork. He paused at one of the closed doors and knocked. When a low, muffled voice bade him enter, he stepped inside, announced Alandra's presence and then moved aside for her to pass.

The personal office was decidedly masculine, with a dark area rug, built-in bookshelves lining three of the four walls, and a large cherrywood desk taking up a good portion of the room.

Dragging her gaze from the impressive surroundings, Alandra turned her attention to the man sitting behind that desk…only to feel her eyes go wide and her mouth fall open.

"You."

"Miss Sanchez." He rose and regally rounded the desk until he stood directly in front of her. "How good of you to accept my offer and come to work for our family."

"You're Prince Stephan—"

"Nicolas Braedon of Glendovia, yes. You may call me Nicolas."

Nicolas. The same Nicolas who had asked her over for a glass of champagne and then invited her to sleep with him.

Her mouth went dry with shock, her stomach clenching and her pulse kicking as though she'd just run a marathon.

How could this be happening?

"I don't understand," she said, her voice faint as she struggled to put her thoughts into words. "Why would you invite me to work for you after the way we parted? All you wanted from me then was…"

Realization dawned.

"You did this on purpose. You lured me here under false pretenses so that I would sleep with you."

"My dear Miss Sanchez," he replied, standing straight as a sword, with his hands clasped behind his back, "Glendovia is very much in need of someone to organize its charitable foundations. And, after seeing you in action, I decided you would be the perfect person for the job."

"And you've changed your mind about wanting me in your bed?" she challenged.

Nicolas studied the woman in front of him, struggling not to smile at her forthright manner and the fury snapping in her brown, almond-shaped eyes. It was a sight to behold, and only made him more certain of the wisdom of the campaign he'd put in motion.

Her rejection of him during his stay in America hadn't dulled his desire for her at all. He had decided, not long after, that since the direct approach hadn't worked, perhaps he needed to go about attaining his goal in a more subtle way.

When it came to Alandra Sanchez, it seemed a bit of seduction was in order.

It had taken him a few days after returning home to land on the idea of asking her to his country for an extended stay. He knew she wouldn't accept if he merely invited her…or if she knew he was extending the invitation, for that matter.

But because they had philanthropy in common, he knew that was the one motive that had a chance of catching her attention. There was also the rather generous bonus he'd included in the employment contract as an added incentive—two hundred and fifty thousand dollars to be donated by him to a charity of her choosing once she'd fulfilled her part of the bargain.

And now she was here, exactly where he wanted her.

Not that she looked even remotely willing to jump into bed with him at the moment. But as with everything else, that would come.

He would see to it.

"I wouldn't say that," he murmured, replying to her question about whether or not he'd changed his mind about wanting her in his bed. "But I am certainly capable of separating business from pleasure."

Without giving her a chance to argue, he continued. "Come. I'll show you to your room, where you can unpack and perhaps rest before supper."

Dropping his arms to his sides, he stepped around her and crossed the room to open the door.

"Don't bother," she replied curtly behind his back. "I'm not staying."

Half turning to face her once again, he maintained a neutral expression. "Don't be ridiculous. Of course you are. You signed a contract."

"Contract be damned." She started for the door, her demeanor icy.

He waited for her to pass, then caught her arm as she marched down the empty hallway. "Are you really willing to deprive one of your favorite charities of a quarter of a million dollars?"

The reminder stopped her in her tracks, and he pressed his advantage. "If you leave, reneging on the agreement, you forfeit the bonus. Stay through the month of December and you will not only be paid the agreed-upon wage, but will also earn a hefty sum to bestow as you see fit."

He could almost hear the gears turning in her head as she weighed her options. Leave, and she would be safe from him; he would have no opportunity to try to lure her into his bed. Stay, and she would be all but walking into the lion's den, but would also end up earning a quarter of a million dollars to fund one of her pet projects. It was a compelling enticement.

The seconds ticked by while she stood in the middle of the hall, wracked with indecision. Once again, he chose to give her a small nudge in the direction he wished her to go.

Moving closer, he placed a hand at the small of her back. She stiffened and pulled away just enough to break the contact.

"Please," he said diplomatically, "allow me to show you where you'll be staying if you elect to remain and fulfill your contract. The family will gather in the dining room for dinner at eight o'clock. I'd like you to be there, if you would, to meet everyone. After that, if you still wish to return to the United States…"

He paused, choosing his words carefully. "I won't say I'll let you go without penalty, but I will be willing to discuss the situation further."

For a moment, he thought she would continue her retreat. And then the rigid line of her spine relaxed slightly and her shoulders lifted as she inhaled a deep breath.

Without turning around, she said, "Fine. I'll stay through dinner."

"Excellent. Come along, then," he replied, careful not to let his satisfaction show as he stepped around her and walked the rest of the way down the hall.

He led her through the foyer and up the curved staircase, toward the west wing. There were more hallways and a second set of stairs before they reached the suites of rooms reserved for guests.

The royal family's quarters were located in the east wing, on the opposite end of the palace. But that was for the best. If his plan to seduce Alandra succeeded, their relationship could be kept almost completely secret, thanks to the relative privacy of the west wing and the fact that she would be the only person in residence there for the next month.

Reaching her suite, he opened the heavy, carved mahogany door, standing just inside to allow her to enter ahead of him. Briefly, he showed her the sprawling sitting room, with its large-screen plasma television and DVD library. Nicolas hadn't known her personal tastes, so he'd ordered the room to be stocked with a variety of choices, any of which she could exchange in the family's entertainment room whenever she liked.

Glancing through the bedroom door, Nicolas was happy to note that Alandra's things had already been unpacked and put away. She was carefully observing her surroundings, and if she was offended that the palace staff had handled her belongings, she didn't say so. She looked pleased with the accommodations, her expressive eyes taking in every detail of the beautifully decorated rooms.

"I'll leave you alone now, to rest or take a tour of the grounds, whatever you like. One of the staff can show you to the dining room when you're ready."

Turning on his heel, he left her standing in the middle of the bedroom.

Alandra watched him go, still seething at his manipulation, and yet not so angry that she failed to notice the handsome, regal picture he made as he exited.

She supposed she should be flattered that a prince wanted her in his bed. Most women would be, she imagined.

The problem was that he hadn't seemed interested in *her,* in getting to know her or starting a relationship with her. His request when they'd met in Texas was to take her to bed for a night—or perhaps a handful of nights. And because of who he was, he expected her to simply acquiesce.

Even if she might have been attracted to him otherwise, that fact turned her off entirely. She didn't want to be some playboy prince's temporary intimate diversion.

With a sigh, she began to explore her rooms,

checking to see where all her things had been stored. Dresses, blouses and slacks hung in the wardrobe. More casual tops and pants had been folded and stacked in the dresser, along with her underthings. And her toiletries had been lined up on the bathroom counter or tucked into the available drawers. Even the books and folders she'd brought, for work and for leisure, had been neatly stacked on a small desk set before one of the windows overlooking the balcony.

She hadn't made up her mind yet about whether she planned to stay, but had to admit that if she *did* decide to fulfill her bargain with the Prince of Lies, the view alone would make her visit feel less like manipulation and more like a paid vacation.

Stepping onto the wide stone balcony, she moved to the railing and gazed out at the ocean beyond. Waves rolled to the shore, bringing with them a gentle lulling sound that could soothe even the most restless soul.

Glancing at her watch, Alandra saw that she still had a couple of hours before she needed to start getting ready for dinner with the royal family. The thought of meeting them caused her stomach to dip dizzily.

But she would deal with that when she had to. For now, she would call home to let her father and sister know she'd arrived safely, and to maybe get Elena's advice about her current situation.

Should she stay or should she go? Should she tell the prince just what he could do with his devious, conniving contract, and walk away from the chance to gift a quarter of a million dollars to a charity that could dearly use the money? Or should she swallow her pride and do what she had to to get through the month?

Four

At five minutes to eight that evening, Alandra followed the maze of hallways on the palace's second floor and found her way to the main staircase. The maid who had come to check up on her earlier had given her general directions to the dining room, and Alandra thought she could find it on her own.

But she needn't have worried. As soon as she reached the stairs, she found Nicolas standing at the bottom, waiting for her.

He was dressed in a dark suit, which made her feel better about her own outfit. She hadn't known quite what to wear to her first dinner with a royal family, so had opted for a simple blue silk dress.

"Good evening," Nicolas said in greeting, watching her intently as she descended the stairs.

Alandra felt a skittering of awareness as his gaze swept her from head to toe. No doubt about it, this man was dangerous. If she decided to stay, she would have to be very careful not to let those blue eyes and his handsome face lure her in and make her do something she wouldn't normally do.

"Good evening," she replied, pausing at the bottom of the stairs.

"May I?" he asked, offering his arm.

She hesitated only a second before accepting, lightly slipping her hand around his elbow.

"You look lovely," he told her as they crossed the marble floor. The chandelier had been turned on, sending bright, twinkling light throughout the foyer and beyond.

"Thank you."

She was saved from having to make further conversation as they reached the dining room. Nicolas opened one of the tall double doors, ushering her inside.

The room was as opulent as the rest of the palace. A long, narrow trestle table ran the length of it, surrounded by heavy, high-backed chairs with seats embroidered with what must be the Braedon family crest. Light trickled down from another chandelier hanging over the table, and glowed from many wall sconces.

The queen and king were already seated at the table, which held intricate place settings laid out for six guests. Nicolas guided her forward, stopping near what she assumed would be her seat.

"Mother, Father, I'd like you to meet Alandra Sanchez. She's from the United States and will be our guest for the next month while she works to help us better organize Glendovia's charitable foundations. And hopefully increase their profit margin. Alandra, this is my father, King Halden, and my mother, Queen Eleanor."

The older man rose and came halfway around the table, taking her hand and pressing a soft kiss to her knuckles. "Welcome to Glendovia, my dear.

We appreciate the work you'll be doing on behalf of our country."

"Thank you, Your Highness," she replied, only slightly intimidated by meeting and speaking with a real live king. "It's a pleasure to meet you."

Turning toward the queen, Alandra noticed that she'd remained seated. And when Alandra approached, she didn't offer to shake her hand.

"Your Highness," Alandra murmured politely and respectfully, pausing before the older woman.

She was greeted with a rather stiff nod, giving her the uncomfortable feeling that she wasn't as welcome as Nicolas and his father would have her believe.

"Please be seated," the queen told her. "Dinner will be served soon."

Returning to Nicolas's side, Alandra allowed him to hold her chair for her before he made his way around the table to the place directly across from her.

A second later, the dining room doors opened again and another couple swept in. It was obvious to Alandra that the gentleman, at least, was related to Nicolas. He had the same build, coloring and facial structure as Nicolas and the king.

The woman had similar physical traits, but Alandra didn't want to assume anything for fear she was a wife or girlfriend rather than a sister.

"Good evening, everyone," the man boomed, smiling easily.

"Mother, Father," the young woman intoned, removing any doubt of her relation to the others. "Nicolas," she added, laying her hands on his shoulders and leaning in to press a kiss to his cheek.

"Menace," he replied, one corner of his mouth quirking up in a grin before he shifted his attention back to Alandra. "I'd like you to meet my younger brother, Sebastian, and my sister, Mia, the baby of the family."

Princess Mia gave a short, harried sigh. "I hate it when you introduce me that way," she told him.

"I know. That's why I do it," he countered. Alandra didn't miss the affectionate sparkle in his eyes or the amusement that lingered on his sister's face as she strolled around the table to take the seat to Alandra's left.

"Our eldest brother, Dominick, is out of the country right now, but hopefully you'll meet him before you leave."

Shaking out the napkin on her plate and placing it neatly in her lap, Mia said, "It's nice to meet you, Alandra. Nicolas mentioned that you would be coming. He says you have brilliant ideas about increasing the amount of funds taken in by non-profit organizations."

Alandra's gaze flashed to Nicolas, flattered by his indirect praise, but he was looking at his sister.

"She's done terrific work with several charities back in the States," he announced.

From his seat across the table, Sebastian said, "That's good. We certainly have our share of worthy causes here on the island that could use a bit of a boost. And it helps that she's quite the beauty." Glancing in her direction, Sebastian winked.

For a moment, Alandra was startled by his brash behavior—in front of his family, no less. Then she realized this must simply be his personality. He was the youngest son, the one furthest in line from taking over the throne, and from the looks of it, a bit of a playboy, to boot.

She returned his good-natured smile before noticing the scowl on Nicolas's face. Her enjoyment fled immediately, replaced by a strange sensation in the pit of her belly. She didn't know whether to be concerned or intimidated, or even amused.

He had brought her here to be his mistress; she knew that. Under the pretense of working for his family, perhaps, but that didn't change the fact that he wanted her in his bed.

However, that didn't explain why he would look so cross at his brother's harmless comment and teasing.

Unless Nicolas and Sebastian had fought over— or perhaps shared—women before. Was Nicolas concerned that his brother would catch her eye before he'd had a chance to seduce her himself?

Oh, that was an interesting twist. And it would serve him right for spinning such a web of deceit to bring her here in the first place.

Servants arrived then to pour glasses of water and rich red wine. When the salad course was served, conversation turned to family and Glendovian affairs. Alandra ate in relative silence, finding the topics interesting, but having few comments of her own to add.

During dessert, Mia and Sebastian asked her about her own family and life back in Texas. She was only too happy to answer, but avoided any mention of the scandal that had driven her away.

"And what are your plans now that you're here?" Mia inquired. "Where do you think you'll begin with the charities?"

Before Alandra could answer, Nicolas interrupted. "That's something I intend to discuss with her at great length, but she's just arrived and I haven't had the chance to fill her in yet on everything she'll need to know." Pushing back his chair, he rose to his feet. "In fact, if you'll excuse us, I'd like to get started on that now."

He came around to her side of the table, taking her arm and giving her little choice but to leave with him. She said her good-nights and followed him across the room.

"Nicolas," the queen called out as he reached the door. "I'd like a word with you."

"Certainly, Mother," he replied in a respectful tone. "As soon as I see Alandra to her rooms, I'll return to the library. We can speak there."

His mother offered an almost imperceptible nod and they left.

With his hand once again at the small of her

back, he guided Alandra to the main stairwell, and they started slowly up the steps. She didn't miss his continued attempts at familiarity. And while his fingertips warmed her through the material of her dress, sending tiny shocks of desire through her system, she had to wonder if it was merely the first phase of his orchestrated attempts at seduction.

Even if it was, it wouldn't work.

She was stronger than that. Nicolas might be charming and gorgeous, his status as a prince alluring, but he had brought her here under false pretenses, and she was not going to be won over.

"So," he began, his voice low and persuasive, "have you had a chance to look over the files I left in your room?"

He had, indeed. A pile of colored folders had been left on the desk, each summarizing a different Glendovian charity she assumed she would be working with if she decided to stay.

"I glanced at them," she said.

"And…"

"You have some interesting organizations set up."

"They're not running as well as they should," he said.

"I noticed."

"Do you think you can fix them?"

That was the problem—she did. Even looking over the files for a few minutes before she'd started getting ready for dinner, she'd had a dozen ideas for improvements. Not to mention raising awareness and drawing in larger amounts of funding.

They were concepts she was excited about and eager to put into effect. But in order to do that, she would have to remain in Glendovia and fulfill the terms of her contract.

"I have some ideas," she replied guardedly, as they turned down the hall that led to her suite.

"Excellent." He waited a beat before continuing. "Does this mean you've decided to stay and work here?"

"I'll stay," she told him. "I'll stay through the month, as agreed in the contract, and at the end of the month you'll give me the bonus you promised."

"Of course."

He might have said more at that point, but she cut him off. "And no matter what your reason for bringing me here, no matter what you expected to happen, I will *not* be sleeping with you. You can cross that little item right off your Christmas wish list."

At that, she turned the knob, spun on her heel and disappeared into the suite.

Five

The door to the library was open when Nicolas arrived. His mother was sitting in one of the armchairs before the fireplace, sipping a glass of sherry and staring at the flames leaping in the hearth. Closing the door behind him, he moved to the sideboard and poured himself a drink before joining her.

"You wanted to speak with me?" he asked, leaning back.

Typical of his mother, she got right to the point. "What is she doing here, Nicolas?"

He didn't pretend to misunderstand the question. "As I told you at dinner, I hired her to help with our charities. She's very good at what she does. I think she'll be a boon to the organizations."

"And that's the only reason," his mother said shortly, eyeing him over the rim of her glass. "Nothing else?"

He took a sip of his brandy. "What other reason would there be?"

"Come now, Nicolas. I may be your mother, and therefore not your first choice of confidante about your love life, but I'm well aware of your… leisure pursuits. Are you sure you didn't bring her here to be your next conquest?"

While his personal relationships were no one's concern but his own, it was hard—not to mention foolish—to tell the queen to mind her own business. Even if she was his mother.

So he did what he and his siblings had done many times while growing up. He looked her straight in the eye and lied.

"Of course not. I take my responsibilities to our country very seriously. As soon as I saw what Alandra had done with the event I attended in

America, I knew she would be a great benefit to our own charitable causes."

His mother narrowed her gaze momentarily, as though gauging the truthfulness of his statement. "I'm glad to hear that. You understand, I'm sure, that it wouldn't do for your little associations to become public this close to announcing your engagement. We both know that you haven't been celibate since you agreed to wed Princess Lisette, but it's important that you keep up pretenses and do nothing to upset her or her family. This marriage will create a very important bond between her country and ours."

A brief second passed, and when she spoke again, both her tone and expression were sharper. "We can't jeopardize that association simply because you can't keep your hands off some American commoner."

Letting another swallow of brandy warm its way through his system, Nicolas consciously unclenched his jaw and forced himself to remain respectful.

"I know my duties, Mother. You needn't worry about me causing any problems with Lisette.

Alandra is a lovely woman, but she's no threat to my engagement, believe me."

"That's good to hear. But just in case you change your mind, or Miss Sanchez suddenly begins to look like an amusing diversion while she's visiting, I have something I think you should see."

With that, she reached between the side of her chair and the cushion and removed a folded piece of paper. She handed it to Nicolas and then sat back, every inch the queen as she awaited his reaction.

Unfolding the page, he found himself staring at a printout of a newspaper article with Alandra's picture. On either side of her photo were two others with jagged edges.

The headline accused Alandra of coming between the man and woman depicted, of being the ruin of a happy home and marriage. He scanned the write-up, which made Alandra sound like a selfish, devious trollop with no compunction about carrying on a torrid affair with a married father of two.

"She isn't one of us, Nicolas," his mother intoned. "She created a scandal in the States and brought shame upon her own family with her promiscuousness. We don't need her here, doing the same to us."

Nicolas tensed in response to both the content of the article and his mother's high-handed warning, then relaxed. This revelation about Alandra surprised him, but didn't concern him. And it certainly didn't change his mind about wanting her in his bed, despite his mother's cautionary warning.

"I appreciate your trepidation, Mother, but I think you're making too much of Alandra's visit. She's only here for a month, and only to help with the charities. Nothing more."

The queen arched a brow, but remained silent, making it clear she doubted his claims. But his life was still his own, and until he had actually taken his wedding vows with Princess Lisette, he owed no explanation to anyone.

Refolding the printout and slipping it into the front pocket of his jacket, he pushed himself to his feet and returned his empty glass to the sideboard before crossing to his mother's chair and leaning down to press a kiss to her cheek. "Good night, Mother. I'll see you in the morning."

* * *

Alandra was up early the next day, ready to get to work and start putting some of her strategies into action.

She also hoped to see more of the island and get *away* from Nicolas. He was dangerous to her peace of mind, and the less time they spent together during her stay, the better.

Carrying a briefcase stuffed with papers, she arrived in the dining room. The family was already gathered and eating. A plate was quickly set before her, and Alandra enjoyed her breakfast until the queen inquired about her plans for the day. Alandra still had the distinct feeling Nicolas's mother didn't like her.

"After studying the notes Nicolas gave me, I thought the local orphanage would be the best place to start," she answered. "I've got an idea directly connected to the holidays that I think will be quite successful, but since Christmas is right around the corner, it's important to get things moving as soon as possible."

If the queen was pleased with Alandra's response, she didn't show it. Instead, Nicolas replied. "I'll have a car brought around to take us to the children's home," he said, pushing back his chair and moving toward the dining room's double doors.

"You're…coming along?" Alandra asked, her words stumbling over themselves as her heart thudded. She really, *really* didn't want to spend the day with him.

He stopped at the door and turned back to face her. "Of course."

Swallowing past the lump in her throat, she tried to ignore the heat suddenly licking its way through her insides. "That isn't necessary."

"But it is," he replied softly. "Glendovia's national charities are my responsibility. I take that duty seriously and intend to work quite closely with you over the next month. I hope you don't mind."

He added the last, she was sure, for the benefit of his family, all of whom were watching and listening attentively. Because it was clear that even if she did mind—which she did—it would make absolutely no difference.

If they had been alone, she might have argued,

but she certainly wasn't going to put up a fuss in front of the royal family.

Forcing the words past her tight throat, she said, "No, I don't mind at all."

His lips curved in a smile that told her he knew exactly how much it had pained her to acquiesce. "I'll meet you at the car, then," he murmured, before walking out of the room.

Ten minutes later, they were seated in the back of a luxurious black sedan, driving away from the palace. According to the map of the island she'd studied the night before, the orphanage was nearby.

She was happy to simply gaze out the window at the passing scenery and mentally review what she hoped to accomplish at the children's home. But she should have known Nicolas would never allow her to keep to herself for long.

"So tell me about this holiday idea you have for the orphanage. I'm surprised you've begun to devise a plan already, without even having visited."

Keeping her fingers tightly wrapped around the folders on her lap, she tore her gaze away from the view and turned to face him.

"The files you supplied gave me a general impression of the home, and the type of event I have in mind is something I've been a part of before. It seems to go over well and is usually successful in getting the community involved."

"Sounds promising," he intoned. "What is it?"

"Basically, we throw a small party where Santa Claus visits the children and hands out gifts, and we invite the press and locals to attend. The goal is to draw attention to the orphanage, reminding people that the children are alone and in need not only over the holidays, but year-round."

Nicolas nodded, his mouth pursed in thought. "Interesting. And who provides the presents for the children, given that your fund-raising efforts haven't yet been put into effect?"

She smiled. "You do."

He raised a brow, and she hurried to elaborate. "Or rather, the royal family does. We'll be sure to mention that to the press, throwing your family into a very positive light. In fact, if this goes over as well as I think it will, you may want to consider sponsoring the event every year. Back home, we've made the visit from Santa an annual event, and it goes over extremely well."

Inclining his head, he said, "I'm sure that's something my family would be willing to consider."

The car eased to a stop in front of the children's home. A second later the driver came around to open Nicolas's door. He stepped out, and a bevy of flashbulbs immediately began going off in his face.

Alandra had slid across the seat to exit behind him, but rather than reaching for his hand, which he held out to her, she lifted an arm to shield her eyes from the blinding onslaught.

"Who are all these people?" she called to him.

He leaned in a bit closer to keep from having to raise his voice. "Just members of the press you were speaking of. They tend to follow members of the royal family wherever we go."

Reaching for her hand again, he said, "Come along. It's time to go in, and you'll get used to the attention."

She wasn't so sure of that. Where she had been happy a moment ago, and eager to get to work, she now dreaded having to step outside the vehicle into the crowd of photographers circling like vultures. She'd had quite enough of that back in Texas.

She'd come to Glendovia to get away from the

media. Now here she was, smack in the middle of the frenzy once again.

Of course, she wasn't the center of their attention this time, which she considered a blessing. But that didn't mean she appreciated having her picture taken without her permission here any more than she had back home.

Drawing a breath, she pushed aside the anxieties swirling in her chest as best she could, then placed her hand in Nicolas's and let him help her from the car.

She stared straight ahead, at the redbrick building they were about to enter. The fingers of her left hand tightened almost desperately on the handle of her briefcase, while she concentrated on keeping those of her right loose and relaxed. She didn't want to give Nicolas a single sign of just how disturbed she was by the reporters crowding around, still snapping pictures and calling out to the prince.

Nicolas smiled and gave a polite wave, but otherwise ignored them as he led her forward. The sea of photographers parted at his approach, and finally they were inside.

Releasing her pent-up breath, she let go of his

hand and stepped away, leaving a safer distance between them. When she lifted her gaze to his, she found him watching her, an amused glint in his eyes.

The move had been an act of self-preservation, and he knew it.

Dammit, he must sense that she was attracted to him, and he probably took it as a sign that he was that much closer to his objective: seducing her into his bed.

"Your Highness," a voice called, and footsteps clacked as an older woman came forward to greet them.

She offered him a small curtsy and smiled at Alandra. "I'm Mrs. Vincenza, administrator of the children's home. We're delighted to have you visit us. I hope you'll find everything to your liking, and we'll happily do everything we can to help you with your efforts."

"Thank you, Mrs. Vincenza," Nicolas replied with a small bow. "This is Alandra Sanchez. She'll be handling the fund-raising plans."

"Where *are* the children?" Alandra asked, scanning the open space, with its center stairwell leading to the upper floor.

"The older ones are in school, of course, and the younger ones are upstairs in the nursery. Would you like to meet them?"

"I'd love to," she answered.

She followed Mrs. Vincenza up to the second floor, with Nicolas behind them.

They toured the nursery, where Alandra played with the babies and toddlers for a bit, then met a few other members of the staff. From there, Mrs. Vincenza showed them the children's bedrooms, dining hall, playroom and reception area.

The reception area, Alandra realized as soon as she saw it, would be the perfect place to set up the Santa Claus event. It was large enough for all the children, the media and any number of guests they might invite. There was even a lovely tree already set up and decorated in the far corner.

She jotted down notes as fast as she could, her mind racing ahead to everything that would need to be done. At the same time, she shared her plans with Mrs. Vincenza, whose eyes lit up at the prospect.

Behind them, standing tall and straight in the doorway, Nicolas listened silently. Alandra assumed that meant he approved of the project so far. She was certain he'd let her know if he objected to anything.

An hour later, she'd finalized the initial plans with the administrator and had a list of tasks to deal with herself. After thanking the woman for her time and enthusiasm, she and Nicolas made their way back outside, through the throng of reporters still hovering on the sidewalk, and into the back-seat of the waiting car.

The vehicle had barely started rolling away from the curb before Nicolas faced her and asked, "How do you feel it went?"

"Very well," she answered, flipping through the pages of her spiral pad and reviewing some of the notations she'd made. "Mrs. Vincenza is eager to help us because she knows it will ultimately help *her,* and even though there's a lot of work to do, I think we've got enough time to set everything up so it goes smoothly."

A small smile touched his lips. "I have to admit, I was quite impressed with what you said to her. You're very good at describing your visions so that others can see them clearly."

Her cheeks flushed with pleasure at his compliment and she nodded a silent thank-you.

"Allow me to buy you lunch at one of our local eateries to show my appreciation for all your hard work. We can discuss what else needs to be done to have everything ready by the week before Christmas."

Although she was starting to feel hungry and certainly could have used a bite to eat, she didn't think it was a good idea to spend any more time with him than absolutely necessary. It would be better to go back to the palace and ask for something to be sent to her rooms, where she could hide out and get some work done *away* from Nicolas.

Without meeting his gaze, she said, "Thank you, but no. I'd prefer to go back and get straight to work."

His eyes narrowed slightly at her refusal, and she almost expected him to argue. But then he turned to look forward and said, "Very well. You should remember one thing, however."

"What's that?"

His eyes returned to hers, bright blue and blazing. "You can't avoid me forever."

Six

For the third time in ten minutes, Nicolas checked his watch. He was standing at the bottom of the main stairwell, awaiting Alandra's arrival, while everyone else was gathered in the dining room, ready for dinner.

But the minutes continued to tick by, and still there was no sign of her.

Spotting a maid leaving the dining room, he motioned her over. "Would you please run up to

Miss Sanchez's room and find out why she's running late for dinner?"

"I'm sorry, sir, but she called down earlier to make her excuses and ask for a tray to be brought to her room."

"Is she ill?" he asked, his brows knitting with genuine concern.

"I'm not sure, sir. She didn't say so."

"Thank you," he said, nodding to dismiss the maid.

As soon as the maid disappeared around the corner, he turned and started up the stairs. Minutes later, he was knocking on Alandra's door.

He heard her call that she was coming, and then the door swung open. She was standing there in a short, turquoise-blue nightgown and a matching robe in some slinky material that made his mouth go instantly dry. Her hair was pulled up and twisted into a loose knot at the crown of her head.

Her lovely chocolate-brown eyes went wide with surprise for a second before narrowing with annoyance.

Noticing that his gaze was inexorably drawn to

the shadowed valley between her breasts, she raised a hand to close the edges of her robe.

"May I help you?" she asked in a tone that surely wasn't often directed toward someone of royal lineage.

Biting back his amusement, he kept a straight face and linked his hands behind him. "I heard you weren't coming down to dinner and wanted to make sure you were feeling well. Is everything all right?"

Her expression softened at his inquiry. "I'm fine, thank you. I just decided to have my meal in my room so I could continue to work."

"You've been working since we returned from the children's home," he said, more of a statement than a question.

"That *is* why you hired me," she replied with a tiny smile.

Her grip on the front of her robe loosened and he caught another quick glimpse of cleavage. His body immediately went tight and hot.

Clearing his throat, he struggled to make his brain work past the thought of stripping her bare and having her writhing beneath him. When he couldn't seem to manage that, he gave a curt nod and headed back the way he'd come.

It took him the full length of both hallways and the staircase to regain his reason and decide on a course of action.

First, he strode into the dining room, where the rest of the family had already been served, and told them he wouldn't be sharing dinner with them. Then he went to the rear of the palace and entered the kitchens, asking that two trays be made up and taken to Alandra's suite rather than only one.

He waited while that was done, and then accompanied the servant as the young man delivered the cart. Alandra answered the door when he knocked, a frown marring her brow when she noticed Nicolas trailing behind. To her credit, she held her tongue as the cart was wheeled into the center of the sitting room.

Glancing toward Nicolas, the servant waited to be told where they wished their meals to be served.

"That's fine, Franc. I'll take it from here. Thank you."

The young man inclined his head and quickly

made his way from the room, closing the door behind him and leaving Nicolas and Alandra alone.

Her gaze skated from the cart, with its silver-domed platters and bottle of wine, to him. "You're not planning on eating with me?" she asked, not bothering with even a modicum of civility as she crossed her arms beneath her breasts and tapped the red-tipped toes of one bare foot impatiently.

"We have a lot to do, as you've said, and I agree that taking dinner in your rooms is a good way to make rapid progress. We'll eat on the balcony," he added, pulling the cart out onto the terrace. "You'll like it out there. Bring some of your files, if you like, and we can discuss them while we eat."

She didn't say anything, but he wouldn't have stopped if she had. Giving her the chance to respond was only inviting a refusal, and he had no intention of being put off.

She followed him to the French doors, still without uttering a word, but stopped before actually stepping onto the balcony.

It was still light outside, edging into dusk, and the bright shades of sunset could be seen on the far horizon. The temperature, normally quite comfortable at this time of year, was even warmer than usual, giving him no qualms about inviting her out in little more than a thin slip of satiny material.

And if she got cold…well, he could think of several ways to heat things up quickly enough.

He moved to the round, glass-topped table outside, and pretended not to be watching her as he transferred their dinner from the cart. In reality, however, he kept track of her in his peripheral view. He saw her fingers twisting nervously on the frame of the open double doors, and her bare toes curling on the threshold rather than taking the step that would bring her out onto the balcony.

"Maybe I should change," she said in a soft voice.

Though he was careful not to let it show, he felt a flash of triumph. She had apparently accepted that arguing or asking him to leave was futile. He was here for dinner, and he meant to stay.

Raising his head, he once again looked directly at her. He wanted her sitting across from him just like that, with her legs bare and the turquoise fabric bringing out the sparkle in her dark eyes.

"What you're wearing is fine," he replied. "This is a casual meal, and we'll be talking about the charities most of the time. In fact, I'll join you in getting more comfortable."

Shrugging out of his suit jacket, he hung it neatly over the back of his chair, removed his tie and rolled up his shirtsleeves. "How's that?" he asked, giving her a moment to study his appearance. "I can remove more of my clothing if you like, but I have a feeling you would consider that a bit *too* casual. Am I right?"

He cocked a brow, silently challenging her to deny it. If he had his way, they would both be naked before the night was over.

For a second, she returned his look with a steady, rebellious one of her own, then spun around and disappeared into the bedroom.

At first, he thought she'd gone to cover herself in battle armor. But she reappeared a moment later, still wearing the same nightgown and robe, and not a stitch more. She was also carrying a legal pad and small stack of folders.

She took a seat and pulled her chair closer to the table, acting as though she was sitting down to a business lunch in a full business suit. But he certainly wasn't going to complain now that he had her exactly where he wanted her.

Following her lead, he lifted the silver covers from both plates and set them aside, then took his own seat across from her. He uncorked the bottle of wine, from one of Glendovia's own vineyards, and poured a healthy portion for each of them.

Nicolas made small talk while they ate. And though Alandra's side of the conversation was stilted at first, eventually she relaxed and spoke to him as easily as she would anyone else.

They'd just begun discussing the plans for the children's home when a knock sounded at the sitting room door.

"That will be dessert," Nicolas announced. Rising to his feet, he slung his jacket over his arm. "Let's move things into the other room, shall we?"

He strolled in that direction, leaving her to follow with her stack of files.

Before the waiting servant had a chance to knock a second time, Nicolas pulled the door open, gestured for him to enter and instructed him to serve the coffee and dessert at the low, square table in front of the fireplace.

While that was being taken care of, Nicolas

lowered the lights, then proceeded to build a small fire in the hearth.

Alandra watched from the bedroom doorway, chagrined to find herself admiring the broad expanse of the prince's back. The narrow span of his waist. The ripple of muscles beneath his crisp white shirt and dark trousers as he moved.

She swallowed hard, feeling a flush of heat flow over her chest, up her neck and into her cheeks.

Noticing Nicolas's considerable physical attributes was the last thing she should be doing. Finding him attractive at all, in any way, would be the kiss of death. A risk she could not afford.

And yet she couldn't seem to tear her eyes away from him.

"Isn't it a little warm for a fire?" she asked as the servant finished his task and slipped silently from the room.

"I thought you might be chilly," the prince replied, turning from the flickering flames and glancing in her direction.

His attention lingered on her bare legs, she noticed, and it took all her willpower not to shift uncomfortably or attempt to cover herself. The only thing that kept her from doing either was the knowledge that he'd noticed the tiny goose bumps beginning to break out on her arms and legs earlier. She was unaccountably touched by his consideration, which was *not* what she wanted to be feeling.

"We won't get too close," he said, dragging the table back from the hearth a few more inches before taking two cushions from the sofa. "Come, have a seat."

He lowered himself onto one of the cushions on the floor and sat cross-legged, leaving the other for her. Instead of sitting across from each other, they would now be much closer, with only one small corner of a rather small table between them.

It wasn't the typical setup for a business meeting. But then, her attire wasn't exactly typical, either. None of this was.

Striding across the room in her bare feet, she set her files aside and curled her legs beneath her as she sat down.

Nicolas poured coffee from a brightly polished silver carafe while Alandra studied the dessert. A fluffy, golden pastry was sliced into layers and

filled with large, juicy strawberries and a deca-
dent amount of rich cream. Her mouth watered
just looking at it.

Because this situation could easily begin to take
on a romantic feel, Alandra immediately started
back on the topic of Christmas at the orphanage,
and didn't stop until they'd made it through the
pastries and a cup of coffee each. To his credit,
Nicolas stuck with the conversation, never trying
to change the subject or insert a level of intimacy
that didn't belong.

His enthusiasm and participation delighted her.
She'd expected him to put in only a minimum
amount of effort, to convince her he'd brought her
to his country for legitimate reasons rather than
simply to become the latest in what she was sure
was a string of lovers.

But he was taking their conversations and the
business of organizing these fund-raisers seriously.
Taking *her* seriously.

It was a welcome change after being made the
butt of any number of jokes and cruel jibes back
home once the rumors had spread that she'd been
sleeping with a married man.

Despite the cup of coffee she'd just consumed, Alandra found herself blinking tired eyes and covering her mouth to stifle a yawn. And maybe she was off her game, maybe her defenses were down, because it seemed sensible, almost natural, to join Nicolas when he moved closer to the fire.

She reclined beside him, letting the flickering flames and the opulence of her surroundings lull her. Keeping company with a gorgeous prince didn't hurt, either, even if she had to steel herself against his charms, his looks, the spicy scent of his cologne.

And he was about as handsome as a man could be. If he weren't already a prince, she would think he should be. A prince or perhaps a movie star.

"What are you thinking?" he asked softly from only inches away.

He had a nice voice, too. Low and slightly husky, it rumbled up from his chest and straight down her spine, causing her bare toes to curl.

If he wasn't a royal, constantly being followed by paparazzi, and if she hadn't recently been slandered and torn apart by vicious rumor and innuendo, she might just be willing to throw caution to the wind and sleep with him, after all. Not become his mistress—that was a bit beyond even her—but spend one passionate, sure-to-be-glorious evening making love with a man who had the power to turn her knees to jelly.

Thank goodness he didn't know that. Thank goodness he couldn't tell exactly what she *was* thinking. Otherwise all her good intentions, her insistence that her presence here was purely business, with no possibility of pleasure being thrown into the mix, would drift away like a wisp of fog on the ocean breeze.

Thank goodness.

"Only that this is nice," she replied. "Relaxing. I should still be working, but I think I'm too tired."

He turned, and she found her own shimmery image reflected in his pupils.

"Would you like to go to bed?"

It was on the tip of her tongue to say, "Yes, very much," before her hazy brain identified the danger his question posed.

"Clever," she said with a chuckle, feeling just tranquil enough to find his attempt to trap her amusing. "But while I would like to go to bed… eventually…I won't be doing it with you."

"What a shame. Although there's always to-morrow."

There it was again, that calm, cajoling tone. The voice that thickened her blood and sent warm, tingling sensations to areas she'd rather not have tingling in his presence.

"I didn't come here for that," she replied quietly.

He was only an inch away now, his heated breath dancing over her cheeks and eyelashes. His mouth looked incredibly inviting, sexy and about seven kinds of sinful.

Surely one little kiss wouldn't hurt anything. One tiny peck to satisfy an overwhelming curiosity.

It wasn't smart. Was, in fact, ludicrous.

Before she had a chance to decide if she could afford a momentary lapse of sanity, Nicolas made the decision for her.

Seven

Oh, my.

He tasted of wine and the strawberries and cream that had been part of their dessert, with a hint of the coffee he'd sipped afterward. Sweet and tart and smoky all at the same time.

It was a heady mixture, but nothing compared to the feel of his tongue sweeping into her mouth, tasting, stroking, claiming.

His hands gripped her shoulder and the side of her face, gently pulling her up. She wasn't sure how it happened, had no conscious memory of moving, but suddenly she was on her knees, pressed chest to chest with Nicolas and kissing him back with equal vigor.

While his hands kneaded and caressed her upper arms, hers clutched at his shirt, desperately holding on and pulling him closer. Her breasts were squashed between them, but she could still feel her nipples beading. Heat gathered and pooled low in her belly, and her heartbeat was a thunderbolt blasting in her ears.

She'd been wrong about keeping her distance, wrong about trying to convince herself she wasn't interested in this man. He was hard and strong and self-assured, and brought to life emotions she'd never felt before, at least not to this degree.

Her fingers trailed upward to tangle in the short strands of his silky hair. The two of them were already mouth to mouth, body to body, as close as they could be while still clothed, but that didn't keep her from exerting a small amount of pressure at the back of his skull and—if it was possible— taking the kiss even deeper.

With a groan, Nicolas moved his hands to skim

the undersides of her breasts. He cupped them in his palms, measuring their fullness and weight before letting his thumbs slide up and over the tight peaks of her nipples.

The caress, made even more erotic by the thin layer of cool, slick material between her flesh and his fingers, gave her shivers.

As she wriggled in his grasp, her knee bumped into the coffee cup she'd set aside earlier. The rattle of the porcelain on the saucer startled her out of the haze of passion and arousal she'd been lost in.

She pulled back slightly, breaking the kiss even though her body cried out for more. Her lungs heaved, straining for breath. Her arms and legs quivered, overcome with a lassitude she couldn't remember ever feeling before.

Good Lord, what had she almost done? How could she have gotten so wrapped up, so swept away by a single kiss?

His hands remained at her breasts, his fingers lightly brushing the rigid peaks. His eyes blazed a deep, dark sapphire in the firelight, no less heated than a moment ago.

Did he not realize she'd pulled away, or was he as blinded by desire as she'd been?

Regardless, she had to stop this, had to make it clear to him that what had just taken place between them was a mistake. A mistake of monumental proportions that could not, *would* not happen again.

"Stop," she gasped.

"What's wrong?" he asked in a ragged voice. Though he dropped his arms to his sides, he clenched his hands, betraying the tension vibrating through him.

"This is not going to happen," she said, though her tone was less firm than she'd have liked. Still on her knees, she inched away, afraid that he might reach for her again and she wouldn't have the conviction to fend him off.

One dark eyebrow hitched upward. "I thought we were off to a fairly adequate start," he replied.

Without looking at Nicolas, she rose to her feet. "I told you before that I didn't come to Glendovia to become your latest conquest. I'm here strictly for business purposes. That kiss was a mistake. It never should have happened, and it won't happen again. Things only got as far as they did because I'm tired and let my guard down."

But Nicolas wasn't ready to walk away, not quite yet.

He also got to his feet, then touched her elbow, stroking the satin fabric of her sleeve. "I could stay," he whispered smoothly, seductively. "Make sure the rest of your evening is both restful and enjoyable. Infinitely enjoyable."

The spark in her eyes let him know he'd overstepped his bounds. She shrugged out of his hold and moved passed him. Wrenching open the door, she stood back, body rigid, and glared.

"Good night, Your Highness," she said, her tone only a shade shy of disrespectful.

If he weren't such a patient man, intent on his goal, he might have taken exception.

But he *was* a patient man, and he knew that pushing Alandra was not the way to win her over, not the way to lure her into his bed. Better to take things slowly, to woo and seduce her properly.

"I'll see you in the morning, then," he said politely, moving to stand before her, giving no indication that her attitude or demands disturbed him in the least.

Though she remained stiff, he took her hand and lifted it to his mouth, pressing a soft kiss to the back of it.

"Thank you for being such a lovely dinner companion, and for all of your hard work on behalf of the children's home. I knew bringing you here was the right thing to do."

With a swift grin, he left the room and strode casually down the hall. A few seconds later, he heard her door close with a slam, and his smile widened.

Alandra Sanchez was a fiery, passionate woman with a temper to match. She thought she was brushing him off, holding him at bay, but her reluctance merely intrigued him all the more.

For the next two weeks, Alandra did her best to avoid Nicolas whenever she could, and treat him with cool professionalism whenever she couldn't.

Nicolas, meanwhile, did *his* best to get her alone as often as possible, to touch her hand, her arm, her cheek on a regular basis, and to romance her into letting down her guard and inviting him into her bed.

So far, she'd remained firm in her commitment

not to be seduced. But she had to admit, at least to herself, that it had been no simple feat.

Nicolas was nearly irresistible. He was attractive and charming, and if he hadn't approached her to sleep with him before getting to know her—which she found gallingly arrogant—she very well might have fallen into bed with him by now.

Sad but true, and rather ironic. If he'd gone about courting her in a more traditional manner, he'd have likely gotten lucky.

Alandra might be considered beautiful by many—a fact of life that was sometimes a blessing and sometimes a curse for her—but she was anything but compliant.

And then there was the continued guilt and humiliation over the scandal that still clung to her name back in Texas.

She'd phoned home numerous times since arriving in Glendovia, and each time she'd asked her sister about the scandal she'd been running away from. Elena had admitted that people were still talking, but the reporters had finally stopped camping out at the house.

But even though the attention had died down,

Alandra knew she'd been right to leave town when she had. She was also even more determined never to leave herself open to disgrace again.

She reminded herself of this, firmly and repeatedly, as she made her way down to the foyer.

In the time she'd been a guest of the royal family, the palace's decor had gone from tidily opulent to brimming with holiday cheer.

The banister had been strung with long, twisting garlands of holly and ivy. Giant wreaths hung on both the outside and inside of all the main doors. And in the center of the foyer was a towering evergreen tree, covered with gold ornaments. A golden angel perched gloriously at the very top.

The holiday decorations were helping Alandra feel more at home. She missed her family terribly, and it broke her heart to think that she wouldn't be spending Christmas with them. But she found it soothing to be surrounded by all this cheer.

She was smiling when she reached the front door, where Nicolas was waiting. Tonight was the Evening with Santa event at the children's home, and he had insisted on accompanying her, despite the fact that she had to be there early. The rest of the royal family would arrive later.

Even Nicolas's mother, Queen Eleanor, had reluctantly approved of Alandra's efforts to aid the local orphanage. She hadn't come right out and complimented her on all of her hard work, or changed her attitude, but the few remarks she'd made about tonight's event had been mainly positive.

Alandra didn't let it go to her head. She knew the queen still disapproved of her.

As soon as she drew close, Nicolas took her elbow, offering a small smile. He was dressed in his princely finery, complete with a red sash running from shoulder to hip, and a number of important-looking medals pinned to his chest.

Alandra's dress was a sumptuous red velvet gown that hugged her curves and left her shoulders and arms bare. She wore classic, understated diamonds at her ears and throat.

"Shall we go?" Nicolas asked, and escorted her out of the palace into the slightly chilly evening air. It wasn't yet dark, but the sun was setting and dusk was well under way.

She had purposely scheduled tonight's affair so

that it could be both a fun party for the children and an opportunity for the adult guests to mingle. Especially since she had invited some very wealthy, influential individuals, whom she hoped would make generous donations.

When Alandra and Nicolas arrived, a crowd of photographers was already gathered outside the orphanage, snapping pictures. Inside, the home was decorated festively. There was a tree in the main entranceway, covered with ornaments handmade by the children. Holiday music filled the air.

After Alandra settled a few last-minute issues, she started mingling with the arriving guests.

The appearance of the rest of the royal family caused quite a stir. Voices hushed, heads turned and people stood frozen as they watched the king and queen.

Leaving Nicolas with his family, Alandra made her way to the other rooms. She began wandering around, double-checking that everything was running properly.

All in all, it looked as though the evening was progressing perfectly. She released a sigh, praying no accidents or crises cropped up to mar an otherwise successful occasion.

Turning back to survey the reception area, she immediately spotted Nicolas striding toward her. Tall and imposing, he seemed to tower over the crowd.

The air caught in her chest. She would have liked to blame her sudden inability to breathe on the tightness of her form-fitting dress, but knew it was all due to Nicolas.

Nicolas, who could stop her heart with a glance.

Nicolas, who made her palms damp and her stomach quiver.

Nicolas, who made her want to rethink her decision not to get any closer to him than necessary during her stay.

Be strong, she told herself, swallowing hard and making a concerted effort to keep her knees from quaking as he came closer.

When he reached her, he gave a small bow and took her hand, his eyes holding hers the entire time.

"Dance with me," he murmured softly.

His tone and princely manner made it more of a command than a request, but she did her best to argue. "I don't think Christmas music is exactly conducive to dancing," she said, glancing about the room. Although there were several couples taking the floor.

"Of course it is."

He tipped his head, as though paying extra attention to the slow strains of a holiday classic. Tightening his grasp, he tugged her behind him as he headed to the clear space at the center.

"Besides, it's my royal duty to set a good example for others, and we want everyone to enjoy themselves, don't we? Isn't that your goal, so that guests will feel more generous when it comes time to start writing checks?"

She could tell from his expression that he was taking pleasure in teasing her, tossing her own ambition back at her in an attempt to get what he wanted. His lips twitched and the corners of his eyes crinkled as he tried to keep his amusement in check.

She might have continued protesting, but it was too late. They had reached a small empty stretch of the hardwood floor, and Nicolas had his arm around her waist, pulling her against him.

He splayed his fingers at the small of her back, holding her in place and guiding her as they swayed in small circles. And just as he'd predicted, others began to follow their lead and joined them, dancing to the holiday carols being piped through the building.

This hadn't been part of her plans for the evening, but it did seem to be having a positive effect. Alandra hoped Nicolas didn't notice, or she might have to swallow her pride and tell him he'd been right.

The song came to an end and they stopped moving, but instead of releasing her, he continued to hold her, staring down into her eyes until her mouth went dry and butterflies decided to take up tap dancing in her belly. Her chest was too tight to draw a full breath, which made her head begin to spin.

She thought, for a brief moment, that he was going to kiss her. Right there, in the middle of a roomful of people.

And she was chagrined to realize that her mouth had opened slightly, that she was both anticipating the kiss and looking forward to it. Yearning for it, even.

With his gaze still locked on hers, he leaned in another inch, until she could feel his warm breath dancing across her skin.

"I can't kiss you here and now, the way I'd like, but I promise to rectify that before the night is through." His voice was low and mesmerizing, washing over her.

Dropping his hand from her waist, he smiled, gave a small bow and then turned and walked away, as though he hadn't just set every nerve ending in her body on high alert.

She watched him go, trying to regain control of her senses. And control of her limbs, which seemed incapable of movement, even as she struggled to get her brain to send the correct signals.

It wasn't until she noticed people beginning to stare that she shook off whatever spell had overtaken her, and was able to take step after measured step to the refreshment table. She poured herself a glass of punch and drank it down in nearly a single gulp.

This was bad, so very bad. He was wearing her down, eroding the last of her defenses.

She was very much afraid that she wouldn't be able to evade him for much longer.

Eight

It was late by the time the evening wound to a close, but as Alandra watched the guests filing out, she was delighted to see that the majority of them had smiles on their faces. Better yet, Mrs. Vincenza had happily reported that she'd received several generous contributions throughout the night, with promises of more to come.

Watching Santa Claus hand out presents to the children had obviously turned a number of hearts—exactly what Alandra had been hoping for. She'd seen more than a few eyes turn misty during the gift-giving ceremony, and many follow the children out of the room and up the stairs at bedtime.

While it hadn't been her main goal, Alandra hoped that tonight's event would result in some much-needed adoptions, as well as added donations.

Stifling a yawn behind her small clutch purse, she watched the door close behind the last guest a moment before she felt Nicolas come to stand beside her.

Although she wasn't surprised that she could sense his presence even before she saw him, it did disturb her. She didn't *want* to sense him. Didn't want to believe that they might be growing that close in such a short time, especially when she'd spent most of the last three weeks avoiding him.

Not that she'd been terribly successful. Nicolas, she was learning, had a way of being everywhere she was, whether she wanted him there or not.

She had to admit, though, that he'd been a definite asset this evening. Not only had he gotten everyone in the room to relax enough to dance to Christmas music, but he'd spent the rest of the night circulating through the crowd to shake hands, kiss cheeks and talk up the orphanage as an extremely worthy charity—or write-off, depending on who he was conversing with.

And she admired him for it. For caring about the children's home and about what he could do to make the fund-raiser a success.

Glendovia was his country, and she had been hired to do a job for it. But he seemed to know that she took her work of organizing charitable events and raising funds for worthy causes very, very seriously. Seemed to know…and in his own way, care.

That touched Alandra more than a dozen roses, a hundred glasses of champagne or a thousand romantic dates ever could have.

He might have taken a wrong first step with her by inviting her into his bed before even getting to know her, but he had taken a few right steps since. Redeeming right steps.

When he took her elbow now, she felt a familiar tingle in every millimeter of skin his fingers came in contact with.

"Ready to go?" he asked.

She nodded and let Nicolas adjust her wrap

around her shoulders before guiding her outside and into the waiting limousine.

Despite the late hour, there were still plenty of paparazzi gathered to snap more pictures upon the royal family's departure. The camera flashes burned her eyes and blinded her vision. She was only too happy to have the car door slam behind her, blocking out the pesky photographers.

When they arrived home, the family said their good-nights before heading for their respective bed-chambers. Alandra wished them all a good night, as well, before turning toward her own rooms.

"I'll walk with you," Nicolas said, catching up with her and once again slipping her arm through his.

She started to tell him it wasn't necessary, but thought better of it with his parents and siblings still within earshot. Instead, she inclined her head, tightened her hold on his arm and murmured, "Thank you."

They walked to her suite without speaking, and she was surprised to find it a comfortable silence. Perhaps because it had been such a long and busy day, and she was too tired to worry about what she should be saying or doing. She couldn't find it in her to be concerned about what Nicolas might say or do, either.

When they arrived, he opened the door, then stood back for her to enter. Crossing the dark sitting room, she turned on a small table lamp, which bathed the space in a yellow-gold light.

Alandra straightened and turned, and nearly bumped into Nicolas, who had followed her silently and was standing mere inches away. For a moment, her mind went blank. Her breath hitched and her heart leaped at finding him so near.

She swallowed nervously and opened her mouth to speak, though she didn't have a clue what she planned to say.

Not that it mattered. Before she could utter a sound or get her brain to function properly, Nicolas had lifted a hand to the back of her neck and threaded his fingers into the loose hair at her nape. He tugged her forward, and she went easily, willingly, like a puppet on a string.

Their eyes met, and in that brief second, she saw passion and fire and desire. Those same emotions caused her stomach to tumble to her toes, and made her feel suddenly light-headed.

Then he bent and lowered his mouth to hers.

The minute their lips met the earth seemed to rock on its axis. Alandra had never felt such heat, such electricity, such an amazing and overwhelming need.

Nicolas's fingers at her nape tightened, while his other hand grasped her hip. Her own hands were on his shoulders, gripping and clawing. She couldn't seem to get close enough.

His scent filled her nostrils, spicy and masculine. As his tongue swept through her mouth, he tasted the same.

She kissed him back with equal fervor, delighting in the way contact with him flooded her senses.

Just when she thought she might expire from pleasure, Nicolas broke the kiss. "Say no," he whispered raggedly against her lips. "Tell me to go. Tell me you don't want this."

He kissed her again, hard and swiftly. "Go ahead, Alandra," he taunted softly, "tell me."

She knew what he was doing. He was challenging her to stick to her declaration that she wouldn't sleep with him during her visit. That she wouldn't allow herself to be seduced.

But, God help her, she couldn't. She wanted him too much to deny it any longer.

To deny him.

Wrapping her arms around his neck, she pressed her mouth to his. The same smoldering heat washed over her again and, with a sigh, she whispered, "Don't stop. Don't go. I do want this."

She expected him to smile—a cocky, self-important response to show her he'd known all along he would win their little cat-and-mouse game.

But he didn't smile. Instead, his eyes flashed with fire, a second before narrowing dangerously.

Bending slightly, he scooped her up, ball gown, high heels and all. His determined strides carried them to her bedroom, where he kicked the door closed and crossed to the wide, four-poster bed.

The room was dark, with only a hint of moonlight shining through the diaphanous curtains on the French doors. It took a moment for her eyes to adjust, but as Nicolas deposited her on the mattress, then stood back to unbutton his jacket, she decided it didn't matter. She could see him just well enough, and in a few minutes she would be touching him everywhere. Feeling him everywhere.

He stripped off his jacket and kicked off his shoes, then loosened the first few buttons of his shirt, keeping his gaze locked on her the entire time.

Not wanting to be a mere bystander, Alandra rose to her knees and pulled off her strappy heels, tossing them aside. She reached behind her for the zipper of her dress.

"No."

Nicolas's low, stern voice stopped her. He took two steps forward to the edge of the bed and ran his hands seductively down her bare arms.

"Let me."

Her stomach muscles clenched as his fingers ran over her abdomen and around her sides, to her lower back. Slowly, he slid his palms up the line of her spine.

His touch burned through the velvet of her gown as his hands trailed upward, and then drew the zipper down. The quiet rasp of the tiny metal teeth parting accompanied their harsh breathing.

When the zipper was lowered, her dress fell open, helped along by Nicolas's large, strong hands. She shrugged and shifted slightly; he pulled it away and dropped it unceremoniously at his feet.

Alandra knelt at the edge of the king-size mattress in her cherry-red bra and panties, and a pair of sheer, thigh-high stockings. Her heart was racing out of control, her nerves skittering like a million angry ants. Licking her dry lips, she remained perfectly still, watching Nicolas and waiting.

He stood equally still, his blue eyes riveted on her face. And then he reached for his shirt, undoing the buttons and pulling the tail from his slacks.

His movements weren't hurried, but they weren't patient, either. He made short work of removing the garment, letting it flutter to the floor while he reached for the front of his pants. There was no belt to slow him down, and with a flick of his wrist, he released both the catch and zipper.

Half-naked, he was impressive enough. But fully naked, he was the stuff of dreams and naughty female fantasies. His arms and chest were beautifully sculpted. A tight, flat abdomen flowed to narrow hips and long legs corded with muscle.

Alandra's pulse skittered and her mouth went dry as she focused her gaze to the area between his thighs. He was impressive there, too.

She didn't know what to say or how to act, so

merely sat where she was and waited for him to make the first move.

It didn't take long. With a single stride, he was with her, cradling her in his arms, while his mouth devoured hers.

Their lips meshed. Their tongues tangled. And everywhere their skin touched, she sizzled.

Alandra curled her fingers into his shoulders, her nails gently scraping. Behind her, she felt him fiddling with the clasp of her bra, and then it came free. She released him long enough to allow him to remove the garment.

Rather than wrapping his arms around her again, Nicolas reached for her breasts, cupping them in his palms, toying with the tight, beaded nipples. All without breaking their kiss.

She moaned into his mouth, pressing even closer. Her own hands roamed over every inch of hot, hard flesh she could reach—his arms, his back, his pectorals and the slim, sensitive sides of his waist.

It was his turn to make a ragged sound of longing when she ran her fingertips over the taut twin globes of his rear, then raked her nails back up to the base of his spine.

She almost smiled. She could feel the desperation rippling through him as he tightened his grasp
on her breasts, deepening their kiss, pressing himself against her belly.

Without warning, he tugged her legs out from
under her, so that she fell flat on her back on the
bed. He followed her down, covering her completely as he trailed his lips across her cheeks, over
her eyelids, along her jaw and behind her ear.

At the same time, his hands worked to remove
her stockings, rolling them slowly down her thighs
and calves, and over her feet. Next went her panties, and she lifted her hips to help him, until she
was blessedly naked, rubbing against him in all the
best places.

His mouth was at her throat now, licking and
sucking and humming, sending little trills of sensation straight to her core. He cupped her buttocks,
bringing her flush with his arousal and turning her
insides liquid with longing.

"You're so beautiful," he murmured, still kissing everywhere he could reach. "Lovelier than I
imagined. And much better than anything I've
dreamed of these past weeks."

She smiled, running her fingers through his hair and enjoying his husky declaration, even if he'd said it to a million other women before. This wasn't about commitment or honesty. It was about lust and desire and untold pleasures, fleeting though they might be.

"You're not so bad yourself," she replied, remembering the multitude of erotic dreams that had revolved around him since she'd moved into the palace.

Grinning, he raised his head to gaze down at her. He leaned in to kiss her, hard and fast, then pulled back, his expression serious. "Tell me you want me," he demanded.

She studied him for a long moment, her eyes locked with his. He was more handsome than any man deserved to be, and when he focused his attentions on her, she felt like the only woman in the world. The only woman he was interested in, at any rate.

And right now, that was all that mattered.

"I want you," she whispered, wrapping her arms and legs around him and holding him tight. "Make love to me, Prince Stephan Nicolas Braedon."

No one had called him by his first name in years, not since he decided to go by Nicolas, after years of his sister referring to him as Nico. He held her gaze for another split second, then pressed his lips to hers. The kiss was hot enough to suck all the air from her lungs and from the room, and she kissed him back with equal enthusiasm.

His hands raked her sides. Then he was caressing her thighs, both outside and in.

His knuckles brushed the triangle of curls between her legs as he began to explore. He stroked and teased, groaning when he found her already damp.

She writhed beneath him as he used two fingers to plumb her depths. She was panting now, and her breathing grew more shallow as he traced his fingertips over the tiny nub of pleasure hidden within her folds.

He touched her there, and she exploded. The orgasm washed over her like a wave of heat.

His smug, satisfied smile greeted her when she opened her eyes. Her cheeks heated at his close scrutiny, and she felt suddenly self-conscious about her wanton response to his touch.

"You blush beautifully," he told her, kissing the corner of her mouth.

He didn't give her a chance to respond, but immediately began caressing her again, his hands filled with magic as they danced across her flesh, leaving no part of her unsatisfied.

The tip of his erection pressed against her opening, and she spread her legs wider, inviting him in. Little by little, he entered her, his heat and hardness filling her. The deeper he went, the more she responded, any signs of discomfort overpowered by the delight shivering through her.

But when he thrust forward in one powerful motion, what had been a minor tenderness turned to a sharp stab of pain that had her gasping aloud.

Nicolas jerked back, brows knit and eyes narrowed as he scowled down at her.

"Alandra," he said, his breathing slightly labored as he held himself perfectly still. "You're a *virgin?*"

Nine

She was a *virgin?*

How in the name of all that was holy could she be inexperienced?

Nicolas's mind raced back over everything he knew about Alandra. All the times he'd been with her, spoken with her, observed her from across a room without her knowledge. Nothing in her demeanor so much as *hinted* that she was an innocent.

And what about the scandal she'd been involved in back in the States? His mother had been only too pleased to share the details of Alandra's indiscretion—a love affair with a married man.

A love affair with a married man that had left her a *virgin?* Nicolas could feel his brow furrowing, the skin of his face tightening as he continued to study her. And all the while he was powerfully aware of their physical connection, of the fact that he still ached and throbbed inside of her.

"How can you be a virgin?" he demanded, his tone brittle and more accusing than he'd intended.

Alandra's eyes grew wider, but passion still filled them. "Forget about my virginity and finish what you started."

To drive home her point, she wrapped her arms around his neck and tilted her hips just enough to send lightning bolts of sensation through his rigid length. He sucked in a harsh breath, using every ounce of willpower he possessed not to start moving, and thrust himself to a glorious but premature end.

His nostrils flared as he took several measured breaths, counting to ten, then twenty. When he could finally speak without groaning or sweating too profusely, he said, "I'm all for carrying on, but as soon as we're done, I *will* want to talk about this."

She rolled her eyes. "Fine. I fully expect you to make my first time memorable, though."

A grin flashed across his face and the mood in the room instantly shifted to a less intense level. There must be traces of royal blood somewhere in Alandra's ancestry. She had the imperial air down pat.

"Oh, darling," he murmured, leaning in to cover her mouth with his, "you can rely on it."

He occupied her with kisses and featherlight touches on her breasts and abdomen. And at the same time, he began to move his hips, slowly and carefully.

By now, her body had adjusted to his size and invasion. Her muscles were relaxed, warm and silky smooth with arousal.

He used long, gentle strokes to start, not wanting to do anything that would hurt or startle her. He hadn't been with a virgin since he himself had been one, and he wasn't sure exactly how to act. How fast might be too fast. How much might be too much.

But Alandra seemed far from intimidated. Her arms and legs were in constant motion, shamelessly exploring his naked body. And she wiggled beneath him, making it difficult for him to hold on to his resolve.

He locked his jaw and concentrated on breathing. His body was alive with sensation, his nerve endings electrified with need and lust and desperation.

"Can't you move any faster?" she panted at last, her back arching and nails raking his damp flesh.

He raised his head to look down at her. Her face was flushed, her hair spread out in a gleaming mass on the pale satin sheets.

"Is that an order?" he retorted, torn between amusement and disbelief.

Her lips curved slightly. "A request. You're treating me like I'm made of glass," she told him, "and I most certainly am not. I may be inexperienced at this sort of thing, but I'm not fragile."

"I don't want to hurt you," he admitted.

She lifted up from the mattress long enough to give him a quick, hard kiss. "You won't. I can take whatever you have to give and then some."

There was only one way to respond. "My pleasure."

His tongue flicked out to tease a ripe pink nipple, and he was smugly satisfied to feel a shudder ripple through her long, lithe form. He kept at it, wetting both tips, suckling them into stiff, rigid peaks.

When he had her shivering in his arms, grasping at his hair and whispering his name, he began to scoot her back, sliding her naked, pliant body across the silky coverlet. Then he grasped her hips and rolled, bringing her over him while he lay flat on his back.

"They say a woman is responsible for her own pleasure. Show me what you want."

Alandra stared down at him, her heart fluttering as she went from being startled by the sudden change of position to feeling empowered by his sensual declaration. His low voice rumbled through her, bringing goose bumps out along her flesh, and he held her hips when she straddled him.

A dozen sultry images of being in the lead and having Nicolas at her mercy played through her mind, and she loved every one.

Spreading her fingers, she pressed her palms on his chest and leaned forward. Her hair fell around her shoulders, the ends tickling his skin. She saw his impressive pectoral muscles jerk, and felt him swell inside of her.

Biting back a grin, she brushed her lips across the line of his jaw. "This is nice," she murmured, kissing her way to his ear. "Having you beneath me, defenseless."

His fingers flexed where he gripped her. "I only hope I have the strength to withstand your torture."

"So do I."

Taking the soft lobe of his ear between her teeth, she tugged gently. At the same time, she rose up on her knees, just an inch, then slowly lowered herself back down. Nicolas groaned deep in his throat, and heat burst in her center.

"Do you know what I really want?" she asked, watching her breath flutter the strands of his brown hair.

"What?" The word came out harsh and strangled as he tried to hold back his base desires.

"I want you to touch me. Everywhere. I love the feel of your hands on my body."

Immediately, he began to explore. His palms drifted to her buttocks, where he gave a little squeeze before sweeping back up the length of her torso to her breasts. Again his thumbs wreaked havoc with her nipples, and with a moan of her own, she kissed him.

Sensations swamped her, raising her blood pressure and making her insides vibrate like the strings of a well-played violin. As good as she'd always thought sex might be, she'd never expected it could be *this* good. That a man—any man—could make her feel both hot and cold at the same time. Make her pant and purr, shiver and shake.

Instinct kicked in and she began to move, her body seeming to have a mind of its own. Her hips canted back and forth, and she rose and fell on his rigid length.

He filled her completely, pressing deep and rubbing with a glorious friction along her hidden folds. Pleasure wound inside her like a spring, from her lips all the way to the apex of her thighs, growing tighter and tighter as the two of them picked up speed.

Feeling as though she were about to explode, she sat up, gasping for air. Her eyes drifted shut and she dragged her nails across his chest.

Beneath her, Nicolas seemed possessed of the same frantic need to plunge and writhe and buck to completion. He met her thrust for thrust, pounding into her on every downward slide. And when that coil of delicious tension building up inside her finally sprang loose, he was right there with her, gripping her even harder and giving a guttural shout of completion.

Alandra's own body shook with climax, rocking her to her very soul before melting into a pile of boneless limbs and damp, exhausted flesh on top of him. His arms slipped around her waist, and where her head rested on his chest, she could hear his heart thudding beneath her ear.

Her last thought before slipping into sleep was that she was glad she'd waited all these years to be with a man. And that when she'd finally taken the plunge, she was glad that man had been Nicolas.

"Now tell me how it is that you got to the age of twenty-nine with your virginity intact," Nicolas demanded.

It was late, the sky darker than before. They were lying in bed, half-asleep after another bout of strenuous, passionate lovemaking.

He'd protested that twice in one night was too much for her, that she would be sore in the morning. But she was having none of it, and had proceeded to convince him otherwise.

Now that she knew the pleasures that awaited her, she had no intention of sleeping the night away. In fact, she was already anticipating the third time being especially charming.

At the moment, however, she was content to lie in his arms, blissfully sated and tucked between cool satin sheets.

"Don't you think my high moral fiber is reason enough?" she replied sleepily.

"It might be, if you weren't more beautiful than a supermodel, and hadn't recently been accused quite publicly of having an affair with a married man."

With a sigh, she pushed herself up on one arm, using her other hand to press the sheet to her breasts. If he wasn't going to let the topic go, she might as well tell him everything and get it over with.

"For the record, it wasn't an affair. Except perhaps in Blake's mind. Blake Winters," she clarified. "That was his name. I met him almost two years ago at a fund-raising event. He's charming and good-looking, and I admit I was attracted to him. He started calling, sending flowers and gifts.

We went out a few times, and he was nice enough, but I didn't think we hit it off quite as well as he apparently did. And I *didn't* know he was married and had a family," she stressed, finally finding the courage to meet Nicolas's gaze.

"Even after I decided not to see him anymore, he wouldn't leave me alone. He kept calling, kept sending presents. He attended my functions and did his best to get me alone. Just about the time his attention started to border on frightening, he stopped trying to contact me."

She shifted uncomfortably, readjusting the sheet around her torso as she went back to looking anywhere but into Nicolas's eyes. "I thought that was the end of it, and then suddenly photographs of the two of us showed up in the press. They were probably taken at the charity events, but they were just suggestive enough to get tongues wagging—especially when a so-called 'source' leaked the information that we *had* been intimately involved. I think it was Blake himself. I think he *wanted* people to believe we were having an affair, maybe even thought, in some sick way, that it would make me go back to him."

She shook her head and took a deep breath, shrugging off the bad memories and any lingering remnants of the shame she'd felt when the story—however incorrect—had broken.

The hair on her nape rose when Nicolas reached out to run the back of his hand over her bare arm. His knuckles rasped along her skin, drawing gooseflesh everywhere he touched.

"Poor Alandra, working so hard to take care of everyone else, but having no one stand up for you when you most needed it."

His words, as well as his tone, surprised her, and for a moment she let herself believe them. A second later, though, self-pity transformed into her usual streak of independence, and she gave an unladylike snort.

"I had plenty of people to defend me," she told him. "Unfortunately, my family is no match for all of Texas high society. In situations like that, the only thing you can do is lie low and try not to do anything even more newsworthy until it all blows over."

His hand moved from her arm to her back. The light stroking lulled her and made her want to curl up beside him once again.

"Is that what you're doing here, in Glendovia?" Nicolas asked softly. "Lying low?"

She snuggled down again, draping herself cozily along his hard length. Resting her head on the curve of his shoulder, she asked, "Is this low enough for you?"

He gave a chuckle, then shifted slightly and pulled her tighter against him, readjusting the cool sheets so that they were both covered from the waist down.

Silence surrounded them, heavy but comfortable. It gave her the chance to listen to Nicolas's breathing and the sound of his heart pumping rhythmically beneath her ear.

"That explains the scandal that surrounds you back in the States," he said at last, his fingers drawing random circles on her upper body. "It doesn't, however, tell me how you managed to remain untouched for so long."

Her mouth twisted wryly, even though she knew he couldn't see her expression. "I'm a good girl. What do you think?"

"I think you're a very good girl," he murmured, his words edged with innuendo. "But no one who looks at you would ever believe you were a virgin."

She cocked her head back to glower at him. "Why? Because I forgot to wear my sweater with the big red *V* on the front?"

"No," he responded calmly. "Because you're one of the most beautiful women I've ever met, and sexuality trickles from your every pore. No heterosexual man could be in the same room with you without wanting you, and I find it hard to believe that one hadn't convinced you to sleep with him before now."

Sighing, she relaxed and settled back against Nicolas. "I don't know how to explain it, except to say that no man has truly enticed me enough. I've dated a lot of men, yes. Wealthy, attractive men. And there were a few times I came close, a few I thought I might be falling in love with. But something always stopped me."

"Until now."

Beneath her ear, his heart seemed to jump against his rib cage and double its beat. Her eyelids, already half-closed, drifted all the way shut, his pulse acting like a lullaby.

"Until now," she agreed, her voice growing faint as sleep began to tug at her. "I guess you could say that your invitation came at a very beneficial time. For a number of reasons."

"One of those reasons being that it gave me a chance to finally get you exactly where I wanted you." With one sinewy arm around her waist, he dragged her up so he could see her face, jarring her into full wakefulness.

Alandra wanted to argue the point or chastise herself for falling so effortlessly into his trap. But right now, in the darkest part of the night, with him lying warm and solid beneath her, she couldn't find it in her to be angry.

Later, maybe, but not now.

Ten

Rays of warm sunlight slanted through the French doors, crossing the carpeted floor and part of the bed, and pulling Alandra slowly awake.

She stretched and yawned and reached out an arm, expecting to find Nicolas asleep beside her. When her hand met nothing but cool, bare sheets, she opened her eyes and blinked until her vision focused.

She was naked and alone in a tangle of pale, wrinkled bedclothes.

Sitting up, she glanced around the room, but didn't find him there.

A sliver of disappointment snaked through her belly. Maybe it had been too much to hope that she'd be able to wake up in his arms. It wouldn't do, after all, for him to be caught sleeping with the hired help.

With a sigh, she rolled out of bed and reached for her robe. Knotting the belt at her waist, she glanced at the clock, her heart pitching when she saw that it was well past 10:00 a.m.

Good Lord, how could she have slept so late?

Not looking forward to the greeting she would receive when she finally made her way downstairs, Alandra showered and brushed her teeth, then started to dress. She wore a simple white sheath with a silver-bangle belt, and white platform sandals. Nothing too provocative, but nothing too dowdy, either.

She wanted to appear cool and confident when she next ran into Nicolas.

Sleeping with Nicolas—a prince, her employer and the man who had propositioned her at their first meeting—wasn't the smartest move she'd ever made. She should have been stronger, more resilient.

Because there was no way she was about to become his mistress for the rest of her time in Glendovia.

Resolve firmly in place, she strolled along the palace corridors and down the wide, curved, marble staircase. There was no one around, not even a servant, making her feel even more awkward about sleeping in so late.

She made her way to the dining room, where she'd spent the majority of her time with the royal family thus far, but the room was empty, long ago cleared of any traces of breakfast. From there, she drifted back across the foyer and down the opposite hallway toward Nicolas's office. She wasn't in a particular hurry to run into him, but he was her primary employer and she was already late getting to work.

The door was closed and she rapped softly, half hoping he wouldn't be there. But he called for her to enter after the first knock.

She schooled her breathing and stepped inside, closing the door at her back. He was seated behind his desk, working, but raised his head to greet her.

Scorching familiarity flashed in his eyes. The look made her heart hitch in her chest.

"Good morning," he murmured, setting down his pen and rising to his feet. "I trust you slept well."

His tone was formal, more formal than she would have expected from the man who'd shared her bed only hours before, with no hint of teasing or double entendre. Yet his gaze consumed her, sliding over her like warm honey, and making her want to do nothing more than relax into it, surrendering her body and her will to him once again.

"Very well, thank you." If he could be this decorous, then so could she. "I'm sorry to be running late this morning. Just because the children's Christmas event was a success doesn't mean I should be allowed to dawdle on the other causes you brought me here to deal with."

She purposely avoided any mention of how they'd spent their time after the Santa gift giveaway, sticking to a professional mode. It was better that way and would help her remain on an even keel.

One side of his mouth lifted, as though he knew exactly what she was trying to do. "I don't think sleeping in a few hours can be considered shirk-

ing your duties. However, if you have ideas for
other fund-raising events, I'd love to hear them."

He waved a hand at one of the chairs in front of
his desk, motioning for her to sit down. As soon
as she did, he returned to his seat.

"Actually, I do have another idea," she said,
feeling some of the tension seep from her body.
Talking business was much better than discussing
last night. "Not for a fund-raiser per se, but for the
development of an organization."

"Really?" His brows rose and he leaned back in
his chair, propping his fingertips together as he listened intently.

"Yes. Back in the States, we have a nationwide
organization that works to fulfill the wishes of ter-
minally ill children. I've noticed that you don't
have anything like that set up here in Glendovia,
and I think it would be a wonderful project for the
royal family to undertake. It would bring you some
outstanding press, and also fill a very real need for
kids who are sick in the hospital or even at home,
with no hope of recovery. I thought we could call
it Dream a Little Dream."

After considering her proposal for several long

seconds, he asked, "And what kind of dreams would we be fulfilling for these children?"

"Whatever they wanted. Their dearest wish, if it's at all feasible. At home, the organization arranges for children to meet their favorite celebrities, spend an entire day at an amusement park that's been rented out just for them and their friends, go for a hot-air-balloon ride or learn to fly a plane. Things that the kids have always wanted to do, but otherwise wouldn't get the chance to because of their condition."

Nicolas returned her grin. "I suppose that could be arranged."

"So it's something you'd consider?" She leaned forward eagerly. "There would be much more involved than simply planning a fund-raising event. We're talking about renting office space, hiring employees, enormous national and possibly international publicity, probably even a press conference or two. And the organization would need continued support long after I return to America."

She thought she saw a flicker of unease cross his face at the mention of her leaving, but it was gone in an instant.

"It's a noble endeavor," he said, shifting so that his elbows once again rested on the desktop. "A good cause, and something that would bolster Glendovia's reputation and its citizens' esteem. I'll have to discuss it with the rest of the family, of course, but I would certainly be in favor of getting the ball rolling."

"Excellent." She grinned broadly, pleased that he was in favor of a project she'd begun to feel very passionate about.

"You have only a little over a week left of your stay," he pointed out.

His mouth was a flat line and his words were curt, as though he found that fact distasteful. The ripple of unease low in her belly told her that she wasn't entirely comfortable with it, either.

When she'd first arrived and discovered exactly who Prince Nicolas Braedon was, she'd threatened to turn around and fly back to Texas, even if it meant breaking her employment contract with the royal family. But now that she'd been here for a while and had really begun to dig into the work, she was enjoying her visit. Enjoying the palace and the country and its people.

She missed her family and was eager to return

to Texas to be with them again, but she was no longer looking forward to leaving, as she had been only a couple of weeks before.

"Do you think that's enough time to establish this organization and get it to the point where it can be turned over to others and still run smoothly?" Nicolas asked.

"I do."

"Even with Christmas coming up?"

"I'll work through the holiday. I was planning to do that, anyway."

Without her family to share in the festivities, and with a multitude of servants who had already decorated the palace from top to bottom, she suspected Christmas this year would end up passing much like any other day.

She'd been prepared all along to spend that time alone in her room rather than intruding upon the royal family's celebrations. At least this way she would have a nice, meaty project to work on and keep herself occupied.

She thought she heard him mutter, "We'll see about that" beneath his breath. But then he pushed himself away from his desk and stood, and in a firmer voice said, "All right. I'll bring it up with the family and see how they feel about it, then get back to you with a decision."

Nodding, she rose to her feet as he crossed the office to hold the door for her. She took a couple of steps in his direction, then stopped.

"Is there anything else?" he asked, noticing her hesitation.

She curled her fingers into fists at her sides, then released them, fidgeting anxiously while she tried to decide whether or not to voice the concerns circling through her brain.

"Alandra," he murmured softly, and started in her direction.

Straightening her shoulders, she met his eyes, stopping him in his tracks. "About last night…" she began, steeling her nerves for a conversation that filled her with dread.

"Yes?" he asked without inflection of any kind.

Obviously, he was in no mood to make this easier on her.

"It can't happen again," she told him quickly and succinctly, as if pulling off a bandage before the pain or aftereffects sank in.

"Oh?" Again his voice lacked inflection, but this time he raised an eyebrow, the only hint that he had any interest in what she was saying.

"No. I realize it's exactly what you wanted, your whole reason for inviting me here to begin with, but it was a mistake and it's not going to happen again."

For a long minute, Nicolas studied Alandra, taking in her rigid stance and stern countenance. He wondered how annoyed she would be if he told her how attractive she looked when she tried to be authoritative.

Deciding not to risk her wrath over that, when he was about to commit a much worse offense to her sensibilities, he pushed the door shut with a quiet click and slowly closed the short distance between them.

"I'm afraid that's unacceptable to me," he replied, raising a hand to touch her hair, which hung straight and silky around her shoulders.

He watched her head tip just a bit away from his hand, as though trying to move away from his touch. And then the tendons of her throat tightened and released as she swallowed, her gaze not quite meeting his.

"It doesn't matter whether you agree or not," she said. "I'm simply telling you the way things are going to be. What happened last night isn't going to happen again."

She sounded resolute. So much so that he couldn't help smiling.

Not that he could hold her response against her. She hadn't known him long enough to realize that he was a man who got what he wanted. He had no intention of giving up so easily or letting her go purely because she claimed their lovemaking last night was a mistake.

He disagreed. Strongly.

Still grinning, he let his hand graze her soft cheek and tuck a strand of hair behind one ear. "I beg to differ. Last night was magnificent."

Her gaze flitted away and a pale pink blush started to creep across her face.

"You have less than two weeks left in Glendovia, and I fully intend to enjoy them. To enjoy you. I know that you'll need to spend your days working, especially if you undertake this new project you've proposed. But your evenings will be free, and I want you to spend them with me, in my bed."

"Absolutely not." She shook her head and took a step back, breaking away from his touch.

As much as he wanted to close the distance between them and grab her up, kissing the quarrel from her luscious, red-tinged lips, he remained where he was, allowing her to believe a few inches of space would keep her safe from him.

A wry smile lifted the corner of his mouth. "You think that I lured you here, created a position for you within my country, to sleep with you for only one night? Alandra," he breathed softly, almost teasingly, "even if you didn't know me well enough by now, you have to realize that no prince would go to such lengths for a single night of sex, no matter how spectacular that sex might be."

Determination straightened his spine and pushed his shoulders back. "I am a bit more dedicated than that," he added, slowly stepping forward. He was encouraged to note that her wide eyes remained locked with his, and she barely seemed to register his approach.

"And now that I've had you, I have no intention of letting you slip away. I wanted to make love to you, and I've done that, but I'm far from sated."

Even as his voice fell, becoming low and rich and seductive, his finger lifted to gently brush against her body. First the curve of her waist and the underside of her breast, then the tender flesh of her upper arm. He kept the contact brief and featherlight, just the tips of his fingers grazing the material of her dress and her bare skin.

And even though he was scarcely touching her, he still felt the shiver of awareness that rippled through her. It sent a jolt of white-hot sensation through his system, gathering and pooling in his groin. He went hard and heavy in an instant, nearly desperate enough to throw her to the floor and make love to her right then and there.

He wouldn't, of course, though it wasn't his royal blood keeping him from doing anything so crass. When it came to being alone in a room with Alandra Sanchez, his royal blood be damned.

No, it was Alandra herself who kept his more base instincts in check. She was already nervous and shy and regretful about what had passed between them last night, and jumping at her now would only cause her to crawl deeper into her shell, to move further away from him.

Instead, he knew he would have to go slowly again, returning to his original plan of smooth, flawless seduction.

Oh, he would have her in his bed again—tonight, if he had anything to say about it. But it would require a bit of persuasion to get her there.

Alandra's chest rose as she inhaled, and her bright, expressive brown eyes drifted closed for a moment, her head tipping down in defeat.

"Please don't do this," she breathed raggedly. "Don't make me do something that I'll hate myself for later."

Her eyes fluttered open and she raised her head to meet his gaze. Her expression was resolute, if somewhat sad.

"I don't want to be Prince Nicolas's secret mistress. A temporary entertainment to be enjoyed while I'm here, then sent away when you're finished with me, never to be thought of again."

Something about her words twisted his heart painfully, and for a second he reconsidered his single-minded determination to have her, regardless of the consequences.

He didn't want to hurt her, didn't want to bring that look of misery to her face.

He wanted to hold her, kiss her, savor her like a glass of expensive brandy.

Why should it be more complicated than that? They were both mature adults, able to make their own decisions and spend time with whomever they chose.

Leaning in slightly, he let his warm breath fan her cheeks as he hovered a scant inch from her lush, kissable lips.

"I don't want you to hate yourself," he murmured quietly. "I just want to be with you. And though I can't change who I am or the prudence my role in this family requires, I don't think it needs to have any impact on our time together. What we do when we're alone, away from the public eye, is no one's business but ours."

He threaded his fingers through her hair, holding her tight and tipping her head back so he could better reach her mouth. He brushed his lips across hers, tasting her, feeling her, absorbing her energy and spirit into himself.

"I only want to be with you," he said without

breaking contact. "And after last night, I believe you want the same thing. You'll have to work very hard to convince me that isn't true."

She didn't answer, didn't pull way. He wasn't even sure she was still breathing. Pressing his advantage, he kissed her again, deeper this time, until her spine bowed against his body and her nails dug into the material of his jacket.

When he finally raised his head, they were both breathing heavily. A shaft of satisfaction rolled through him at the cloudy, unfocused look in her eyes.

"Very hard," he whispered.

Eleven

It was beyond difficult to convince Nicolas that she didn't want him. So impossible, in fact, that she'd given up trying.

How could she claim she wanted nothing to do with him when one touch of his hands or mouth melted her insides like a pot of chocolate fondue?

He'd discussed the idea for the Dream a Little Dream Foundation with his family, even asking Alandra to draw up an official proposal he could take to them. He'd also done a bit of research on his own into its American counterpart, so he could show them what the end product of such an endeavor might be like.

Reaction so far had been positive, and she and Nicolas had been working together on a daily basis to plan things in more detail, crossing all the t's and dotting all the i's. Once the king and queen approved, as well as the board of Glendovian officials who oversaw this type of thing, she would be given the freedom to get the ball rolling on establishing the foundation.

Daylight hours were not her problem. She had plenty to do to keep her busy, and managed to make sure she wasn't alone with Nicolas any more than necessary.

The door of his office stayed open while they were working, and if for some reason it was closed, she found a way to get it open again. If they were alone and things began to feel too tense, too dangerous, she'd make an excuse to get someone else into the room with them.

It was nighttime that caused her the most anxiety. After dinner, when Nicolas would walk her back to her rooms…holding her hand, standing too close, leaning into her at the door.

He kissed her cheek or sometimes her lips. Stroked her hand or shoulder. And always, *always* his eyes blazed with the clear desire to sweep her up in his arms and cart her off to bed.

She prayed he'd never figure out how very often she wished he would do just that.

Obviously, she wasn't safe around him, and she didn't know how she was going to make it another ten days without either giving in or going crazy.

Ten more long, arduous days and she could fly home, fly away to safety.

For some reason, though, that knowledge didn't comfort her as much as she would have hoped. In fact, it almost saddened her.

But that was an emotion she refused to examine. Her entire existence had been turned upside down, and as soon as she arrived home, life would begin to right itself and return to normal.

She hoped.

For now, though, it was late, and she'd thankfully managed to survive another day, another dinner, another long, excruciating walk back to her suite.

She'd changed into a pair of comfortable black satin pajamas and was ready to climb into bed when a soft knock sounded on the sitting room door.

A petite young woman in the uniform of the palace's household staff stood on the other side.

"Miss," she said, bobbing a slight curtsy. "Prince Nicolas sends this message and requests an immediate response." She held out a square envelope.

It was Nicolas's official stationery, Alandra saw, with her name scrawled in his expansive script across the front, and a dab of wax sealant pressed to the back.

Whatever was inside, she suspected, was either very important or very private.

Running a finger under the flap of the envelope, she broke the seal and removed the folded sheet of paper.

Alandra—
Your presence is required at a very important meeting concerning Dream a Little Dream. We fly to the other side of the island tomorrow morning. Pack for at least one night. Be ready to leave at 7:00 a.m.
Nicolas

She wasn't sure exactly what response he was awaiting, since he didn't seem to be giving her much choice in the matter. He hadn't asked if she wanted to go or would be willing to go, or was even able to go…he'd simply told her to be ready.

Refolding the note, she stuffed it back in the envelope before returning her attention to the servant. "Tell the prince I'll be in the main foyer by seven o'clock. Thank you."

The woman nodded and hurried off, ostensibly to deliver the message. More like announce Alandra's compliance, she thought crossly as she shut the door and headed back to the bedroom.

Though she wasn't particularly happy about this new development, she dragged an overnight bag from one of the closets and began to pack.

By the time she'd finished, she was truly exhausted. Climbing into bed, she hoped for a good night's sleep.

She would need all the rest she could get if she was going to be alone with Nicolas—away from the palace. Overnight.

She met Nicolas outside the palace at exactly 7:00 a.m. The entire place, inside and out, was decorated to the nines in anticipation of the Christmas Eve party the royal family was hosting in only two days' time.

"Good morning," he said.

"Good morning."

"I'm glad you were able to accompany me to this meeting," he told her once they were inside the car and heading down the driveway.

"I didn't have much choice in the matter, did I?" she replied, avoiding his gaze by staring out the window.

"You always have a choice."

She turned her head, meeting his blue eyes. "Well, your note didn't seem to *ask* if I'd like to go with you."

"I was afraid that if I did ask, you would have said no," he confessed.

"Of course I wouldn't have said no. As long as this meeting actually does concern the Dream a Little Dream Foundation. Or did you just say that to get me alone and away from the palace for a few days?" she asked quietly.

A moment passed before he responded. "This trip *is* about the foundation, and though I could probably handle things well enough on my own, I think it's important that you're there. I think you'll be glad you came."

He paused again, letting the silence fill with tension as his sharp gaze bored into hers. "But I'm also quite happy to get you away from the palace and to myself. I think you'll be glad for that, too—eventually."

His voice lowered to a warm, honeyed tone, and it took all of Alandra's willpower not to suck in a deep breath of air to replace what had gotten stuck in her throat.

She should be angry. He was manipulating her again, moving her how and where he wanted her in an effort to change her mind about sleeping with him.

One thing could be said for Nicolas Braedon— he knew what he wanted and didn't take no for an answer.

She didn't want to admit it, not even to herself, but the truth was his single-minded determination to seduce her made her feel…special.

It wasn't her intention to play with him, to turn this…whatever it was between them…into a game, but she suddenly realized she was enjoying herself. She enjoyed knowing that he wanted her.

Instead of arguing or giving in too soon, she merely shrugged and said, "I guess we'll have to wait and see."

The flight to the other side of the island was a short one, and they went straight from the small private airstrip to the office where the meeting was scheduled.

Alandra was stunned to learn that they weren't simply meeting with a few people *about* establishing the new foundation, but were meeting with many people to actually get the organization up and running.

As the morning meetings progressed, she realized Nicolas had been right. She was glad she'd come along.

She was also thrilled with the amount of progress they were making in such a short time. Over a working lunch she met wonderfully enthusiastic people raring to get started. She had no doubt they would do an excellent job of running the organization, whether she was there or not.

She and the prince said goodbye to the future Dream a Little Dream staff at five, and Nicolas instructed his driver to take them to a hotel where the royal family kept a suite of rooms.

Alandra wasn't taken aback, and she wasn't upset. In fact, she belatedly realized she'd expected as much. After her little revelation in the car on the way to the airport that morning, she even found herself looking forward to what the evening might bring.

The royal suite was gorgeous. Nicer, even, than her rooms at the palace.

The walls, carpeting and drapes were all done in varying shades of blue, with touches of white and tan. A set of dark mahogany French doors opened onto a small lanai overlooking the city and the coastline beyond. One of the doors was open, allowing a cool breeze to ruffle the long, diaphanous curtains, bringing in the salty scent of the sea.

"Are you hungry?" Nicolas asked, stepping to a desk that held a thick, black binder of hotel amenities.

She nodded, moving slowly in his direction as she continued to take in her surroundings. She wondered if she should bother unpacking, or simply live out of her overnight bag.

"I'll have something brought up," he said, flipping through the room service menu and then calling down to order what sounded like a veritable buffet of appetizers and entrées. Before hanging up, he asked for a bottle of their best wine, and strawberries with fresh whipped cream for dessert.

"We have about thirty minutes before the food arrives." Loosening his tie and shrugging out of his suit jacket, he draped both over the back of a chair as he crossed the room. "Would you care to change into something a bit more comfortable before it gets here?"

His gaze raked her from head to toe, raising gooseflesh every inch of the way.

She knew when to admit defeat—and when to enjoy a very handsome man who was more than willing to pleasure and worship her, if only for a short while.

"Do you have any special requests?" she asked, slowly removing her watch, and then her earrings.

Next she raised a hand to the top button of her blouse, slipping it through its hole.

His eyes followed her actions intently, glittering with longing and sending sparks of awareness through her.

"Naked works for me," he murmured, his voice gravelly with desire.

She chuckled, feeling a thrill of empowerment swelling in her veins. "Not just yet, I don't think," she said, turning on her heel and heading for the bedroom. "I wouldn't want to shock the waiter when he arrives."

"If he sees you naked, I could have him killed."

She laughed again, facing him with her hands on the knobs of the double bedroom doors.

"Let's not turn this trip into a crime spree just yet. Not if we can help it," she told him as she swung the doors closed. "I'll see what I can come up with on my own."

She stayed in the bedroom until she'd heard the room service waiter deliver dinner and leave again.

Opening one door a crack, she saw Nicolas standing before the round table on one side of the sitting area. It had been set with an array of dishes and stemware.

Stepping the rest of the way into the room, she paused and waited for him to notice her. When he did, his hand froze on the silver serving lid he'd been about to raise, and his gaze zeroed in on her like a heat-seeking missile.

She'd changed into a long black nightgown with spaghetti straps and lace-lined slits running from ankle to midthigh on each side. Her feet were bare, her red-tipped toes peeking out from beneath the hem of the nightie, and she'd combed her hair out to fall in a straight, silky curtain around her shoulders. The look on Nicolas's face told her how completely he appreciated her efforts.

"It's not naked, but I hope you approve."

He swallowed hard. "Very much so. I didn't think it was possible, but that gown may just be better than full nudity."

An amused smile tugged at her lips. "I'm glad you said something. Now I know not to take it off, no matter how much you beg."

"Princes don't beg," he informed her, stalking slowly toward her.

"No?" she asked, her mouth going suddenly dry.

"No."

He was standing in front of her now, close enough to touch, but keeping his arms at his sides. Her heart was pounding in her chest and she had to fight the urge to wiggle nervously.

"What do princes do, then?" she asked, her voice husky with growing pleasure.

Reaching out, he stroked the back of his fingers across her cheek. "It would be better if I showed you."

"Won't dinner get cold?"

"Do you care?"

Twelve

Late that night, Alandra lay in bed, wrapped snugly in Nicolas's arms. She couldn't have been more physically comfortable and sated…but her emotions were in an uproar.

She had done the very thing she'd sworn not to—she'd become Nicolas's lover.

As disturbing as that was, as much as it made her question her own character, it wasn't what had her teetering on the edge.

She'd realized not an hour before—while

Nicolas was kissing her, stroking her and making her sigh—that she was falling in love with him.

She swallowed hard, blinking to keep the moisture collecting at the corners of her eyes from spilling over. Beneath her cheek, Nicolas's chest rose and fell with his easy breathing.

This was bad. So bad. An affair was one thing. But how was she supposed to leave for home with a smile on her face if her heart was left behind, broken and bleeding?

How was she supposed to pretend that what had passed between them was just a holiday fling, when it had become so much more than that to her?

Nicolas shifted slightly in his sleep, causing her breath to catch. When he didn't wake up, she relaxed, feeling a bit steadier.

Since she knew she was merely a temporary distraction for him, and that he didn't share her newfound sentiments in the least, she would simply have to deal with the situation as best she could. Hide her feelings. And then, when the time came, she would walk away.

Closing her eyes, she began to drift off, telling

herself to get used to the pain squeezing her heart. It was going to be with her for a long time to come.

They returned to the other side of the island the following morning, Christmas Eve, with many hours to spare before the family's annual holiday party. Nicolas had made certain Alandra knew she was to attend, though she wasn't entirely looking forward to it.

Stepping off the plane, they were accosted by a large group of reporters, all snapping pictures and screaming out questions. She had trouble making out the exact words, and Nicolas bustled her into the back of the waiting limousine before she could decipher them.

"What was that about?" she asked breathlessly as the car shifted into gear and headed toward the palace.

He shook his head. "The press probably caught wind of our travels and are trying to see if it's worthy of front page news."

The media attention still seemed odd to her, since the trip had been business-related and the palace likely would have already delivered a press release outlining the prince's plans. But she pushed aside her misgivings and relaxed in the comfortable, stuffed leather seat.

When they arrived at the palace, the queen was waiting for them in the main foyer. Her face was pinched, her mouth set in a flat, angry line. Though she didn't raise her voice, the disapproval in her tone was clear as glass.

"In the library," she snapped. "Now."

Nicolas and Alandra exchanged a questioning glance, then slowly followed in the queen's rapid-fire footsteps.

As soon as they stepped into the library and closed the door behind them, Eleanor spun back around, holding a newspaper in her shaking hands. *"What,"* she demanded through clenched teeth, "is the meaning of this?"

Alandra stood perfectly still, stunned by the queen's obvious displeasure, but unsure of the cause. As hard as she tried, she couldn't make out the headline of the article being waved between them.

Seemingly unfazed by his mother's mood, Nicolas reached for the paper. There, taking up nearly all of the top half of the front page was a close-up photo of Nicolas and Alandra. They were standing on the balcony of the hotel suite, caught in an unmistakable embrace.

The photo had to have been taken after they had made love, then gone out on the balcony for a breath of fresh air…only to end up kissing for long, stolen moments before drifting back inside to make love again.

Alandra's cheeks flamed at both the memory and the knowledge that someone had been out there, snapping pictures of a very private moment.

Above the photo, sending a wave of nausea through her stomach, was a bold, glaring headline that declared her Prince Nicolas's American Tart.

Nicolas muttered a dark curse beneath his breath and lowered the newspaper.

Still vibrating with anger, the queen said, "You and your little…*American* are on the front page of every newspaper in Glendovia. I told you, Nicolas. I *told* you not to get involved with her, that she would only bring shame and embarrassment to our family."

The sick sensation clawing at Alandra's insides grew worse. She'd come to Glendovia to get away from one scandal, only to find herself smack in the middle of another.

And this one was even worse, because now it was true. She hadn't had an affair with Blake Winters, as the American press had claimed, but she *had* been sleeping with Nicolas.

"Mother," Nicolas growled.

His jaw was clenched, and the single word was clearly a warning. One the queen chose to ignore.

"Princess Lisette arrived less than an hour ago—in tears. She's crushed, and her parents are furious. Do you have any idea how this indignity will affect your upcoming nuptials? If she backs out of the engagement, our family's ties with hers will be fractured. The political future of Glendovia could be in peril."

"I think you're overreacting," Nicolas remarked, but it was obvious from his expression that the entire situation had him concerned.

Alandra's brain had gotten stuck on two words that made her heart feel as though it were being squeezed in a vise.

She turned her head toward Nicolas. "You're engaged?" she asked.

"It's not what you think," he said shortly. "I can explain."

But she didn't want to hear explanations, excuses, lies or more of the persuasive and creative arguments he seemed only too talented at spinning.

It was her turn to shake her head as she backed away.

"I'm sorry," she murmured shakily, directing her apology to the queen, not Nicolas. She had nothing to apologize to him for.

"I'm sorry," she said again, "I didn't know he was betrothed. I certainly didn't come here with the intention of getting involved with Nicolas. I would never have knowingly brought any embarrassment or undue attention to your family. I hope you can believe that."

The queen's pinched expression did not change as she turned to look at her son. "I'll expect the two of you to keep your distance from now on. You will conduct yourselves with the utmost decorum and stay as far from each other as possible while we rectify this situation. Is that understood?"

Nicolas looked as though he wanted to argue, but Alandra was already nodding. She blinked to hold back tears of humiliation, even as she licked her dry, parched lips.

"You may go," Eleanor told her, clearly dismissing her. "And you," she said to Nicolas, "will speak with Lisette immediately, and do your best to repair whatever damage has been done. Is that understood?"

Alandra slipped out of the office, closing the doors behind her without waiting to hear Nicolas's reply, and hurried across the parquet floor for the stairs. All she wanted was to get away, get back to her rooms, where she could be alone. What a fool she'd been. Again.

Standing in the doorway of her suite, Alandra took one last look around to be sure she hadn't left anything behind. All had been erased.

Closing the door quietly behind her, she walked down the hall, pulling her wheeled carry-on behind her. Instead of heading for the front of the palace, where guests would be arriving for the Christmas Eve party, she slipped toward the back, where a car was waiting to take her to the airport.

Leaving now meant giving up the hefty bonus

Nicolas had promised for the charity of her choice, but she simply couldn't stay. She wanted to go home, where she would be surrounded by family. Where she could hopefully hide and start to heal.

At the moment, the pain in her heart didn't feel as though it would ever go away, but she was hopeful. Hopeful that the sooner she left Glendovia, the sooner she could put this entire incident behind her. That the farther she could get from Nicolas, the faster she would begin to forget that she'd let herself fall in love with him—and that he'd been lying to her the entire time.

"Thank you for all of your help," she said to the woman who had helped her arrange for the car and a flight back to the United States.

Alandra handed her a stack of thick files and paperwork, with a separate sheet of stationery clipped to the outside. Despite her eagerness to leave, she had taken the time this afternoon to make certain the foundation wouldn't be left in the lurch.

"Please see that Prince Nicolas gets this. It should be everything he needs to continue with the Dream a Little Dream project."

The woman nodded and offered a small curtsy. "Yes, miss. It was a pleasure to meet you."

"Thank you," Alandra said, swallowing back tears. In only a few short weeks she had grown unaccountably close to the palace staff and was sincerely going to miss them.

With her throat too clogged to speak another word, she walked to the waiting vehicle and climbed in the back. It was dark outside, and too dark to see much of anything through the tinted rear windows. But even so, as the car rolled slowly away from the palace, Alandra kept her gaze focused straight ahead, not wanting to catch even one final glimpse of the site where she'd experienced both an incredible amount of happiness and an incredible amount of heartache.

Nicolas kept his expression impassive throughout the night, giving no hint of his dark, foul mood. He was only too relieved when the Christmas party drew to an end and he was able to slip away from his family and their guests.

He muttered a curse through gritted teeth as he made his way down the long hallway to Alandra's rooms. This was *not* the way he'd hoped things would turn out between them, or how he'd intended her visit to Glendovia to draw to a close.

When he reached her suite, he knocked lightly, then opened the door and entered without waiting for her response.

The lights were on and he heard noises coming from the bedroom, but something seemed oddly out of place.

"Alandra?" he called, striding in that direction.

He pushed open the door, immediately taking in the stripped bed and the lack of Alandra's personal items, which had been scattered about the first night he'd spent with her. A second later, a maid appeared in the bathroom doorway and gave a little squeak of surprise.

"Your Highness," she said, bowing her head.

"Where is Miss Sanchez?" he asked, frowning in consternation.

"I'm sorry, sir, but she's gone. Left just before the party began."

"She's gone?" he repeated, feeling as though his feet had been swept out from under him.

"Yes, sir. I believe she left something for you, though, with Delores. Shall I get her for you?"

"Yes, thank you. Have her bring it to my office, if you would, please."

"Yes, Your Highness."

The maid rushed around him and out of the room. Nicolas trailed behind at a much slower pace, taking a back stairwell to the first floor and heading for his private office. Ten minutes later, Delores arrived. She had a stack of folders in her arms.

"Miss Sanchez left these for you, sir," she said, handing them across the desk to him.

He thanked her, waiting until the servant had gone before opening the note on top of the pile. Alandra's letter was oddly lacking in emotion, simply explaining that she couldn't stay any longer, regardless of the requirements of her contract, now that she knew he was engaged to be married and those pictures had become public. The files, he discovered, held pages upon pages about the Dream a Little Dream Foundation.

He should have expected that she wouldn't want to leave unless she was sure all of the project details were in his hands, and that the establishment of the organization would move forward as planned.

The problem was, he hadn't expected her to leave at all. Not without talking with him, letting him explain.

He should have told her about Lisette in the beginning. Should have let her know that it was an arrangement made by his parents and not necessarily his choice. That even though he was betrothed to the princess, they had never been physically involved.

Lisette and his mother would be delighted to learn of Alandra's departure. Without her presence in Glendovia, the scandal of their affair would die a quick death, and life as they knew it could move on, including plans for his upcoming wedding.

He only wished he felt the same. Instead, he found himself wanting to charge down the hall and be driven to the airport, follow Alandra all the way back to Texas.

If only she'd given him a chance to explain.

With a sigh of regret, he crumpled her note.

It was better this way, he told himself as he left his office and strolled slowly to his rooms on the second floor. Now that Alandra was gone, things could return to normal. He could get back to the matters at hand without being preoccupied with thoughts of making love to her just one more time.

Yes, it was better this way. Better for everyone.

Thirteen

The noise from the back of the room buzzed in Alandra's ears. She really didn't want to do this.

After arriving home from Glendovia in the middle of the night—Christmas night, no less—she'd done her best to get her life back on track. News of her affair with Nicolas had yet to trickle back to the States. But if anyone in her immediate circle had heard about the affair they'd wisely chosen to ignore the gossip.

Everyone except her sister. Elena had waited

until they'd gotten home from the airport to say anything, but she'd known instinctively that something had sent Alandra running back to Texas.

The minute they were alone, Alandra had broken down and told her sister everything, pouring her heart out about the situation and how she'd unwisely fallen in love with a man she could never have. And as always, her sister had understood. She'd listened and offered appropriate responses at appropriate times, but never acted as though she thought Alandra had been a fool to get involved with Nicolas in the first place.

Elena was also the one who'd encouraged her most strongly to throw herself back into her work, when Alandra had wanted nothing more than to curl up in a ball and hide under the covers for the next month or two.

Which was how she'd ended up backstage at the Gabriel's Crossing Country Club. Long before she'd left for Glendovia, she had not only helped finalize the evening's New Year's Eve bachelorette auction, but she'd somehow allowed herself to be roped into being one of the bachelorettes, as well, and now they were holding her to her promise.

The event was in full swing. Six other women had already pranced down the runway to a smattering of applause and generous, good-hearted bidding by the interested bachelors in the audience. Two more ladies were set to take their walks, and then she would be next.

She swallowed hard, taking deep breaths to keep from drowning in panic. This wasn't her idea of a good time. She far preferred to remain behind the scenes at these events. Being the center of attention—especially with all of the publicity that had surrounded her lately—made her knees shake and her teeth rattle.

One bachelorette down, one to go.

"Alandra," a woman who was helping out backstage called in a loud whisper. "Get ready, you're next."

Oh, God, oh, God, oh, God.

For a brief second, she wondered how far she would be able to run in four-inch heels. She probably wouldn't get far, but it was still worth a try.

Inhaling deeply and praying she wouldn't trip over the hem of her gown, she started slowly down the makeshift runway to the sound of scattered clapping and the voice of the master of ceremonies, who extolled her many feminine virtues and outlined the details of the date she'd agreed upon beforehand.

She felt like an animal at a zoo, on display for the whole world to gawk at and appraise. And as she neared the end of the runway, her stomach plunged when she realized that not a single bid had been called out yet.

Oh, Lord, please let the floor open up and swallow me whole, she thought.

At the end of the runway, she stopped and posed, more from embarrassment than any wish to act like a supermodel. Except for the MC asking if there were any bids, any bids at all, the room had fallen into utter silence. The scandals, it seemed, hadn't quite died down, after all.

Alandra blinked, feeling the stares of a hundred people boring into her like laser beams. She was just about to turn in disgrace and walk back to the curtain when a voice rang out from the rear of the room.

"Two hundred and fifty thousand dollars."

Her heart stopped, and she strained to see who had made such an outrageously extreme offer. The rest of the crowd did the same, twisting in their seats for a glimpse of the mystery bidder.

Elated, the MC quickly declared Alandra "sold!" to the gentleman at the rear of the room. At that announcement, the bidder started forward.

As the bachelor walked toward her, he moved into better light, and Alandra's heart stopped again, but for a much different reason this time.

Nicolas, in all his royal finery, stepped through the crowd. A couple of hulking, black-suited bodyguards trailed behind, making his presence stand out all the more.

She opened her mouth to breathe his name, but no sound emerged.

At the end of the raised walkway, Nicolas stopped to gaze up at her. He stretched out a hand, his face showing nothing as he reached toward her.

"May I?" he asked in that rich, deep voice that sent shivers down her spine.

Without conscious thought, she put her hand in his and let him lift her bodily from the runway, then lead her back through the crowded room to the rear of the building. She let him take her away from her own event, away from the gawking stares and curious onlookers, to the limousine that waited just outside, on the paved country club driveway.

Nicolas handed her inside and climbed in behind her, allowing the driver to close the door. A second later, she heard the driver's door slam shut, but the partition was up, and she knew that for all intents and purposes, she and Nicolas were alone.

"What are you doing here?" she asked when she finally regained her senses and found her voice.

"I bought you," he replied easily, purposely ignoring the seriousness of her question.

The look in her eyes must have warned him he was skating on thin ice, because he sighed and shifted lightly on the leather seat.

"There have been some developments back in Glendovia since you left. Positive ones, in my estimation. For one, plans for the Dream a Little Dream Foundation are moving forward. We're estimating a March first start date for having everything up and running."

"I'm glad," she said softly. She was happy that things were moving smoothly with the plans she'd put into effect before leaving. But she doubted

Nicolas had flown all the way to America just to deliver an update.

"For another, I've reconsidered my original desire to have you as my mistress." His eyes met hers then, hard and unyielding. "It was shortsighted of me to believe that having you only temporarily would ever be enough."

Sliding across the seat, he wrapped his arms around her and tugged her against his chest. She went willingly.

"I've missed you, Alandra," he whispered against her hair. "I tried to forget you, tried to put you out of my mind and move on with what I knew I had to do."

His hands stroked her back, her neck, the side of her face. "But I couldn't go through with my engagement to Lisette when only one woman filled my heart. You're the one that I want, Alandra. Not as my lover or mistress, but as my wife."

Tipping her head back, she met his gaze, searching his startling blue eyes for the truthfulness in his words. And still she was afraid it was all a dream, that she would wake up to find herself alone, in her bed, with Nicolas nowhere around.

"I broke my engagement to Princess Lisette. It's caused a few hurt feelings and political problems between our two countries, but nothing that won't heal in time. And I've informed my family—my mother, especially—that I was coming to get you and wouldn't return unless you were at my side."

He slid his fingers through her hair, tugging loose the elaborate knot at the crown of her head and dislodging the tiny diamond clips holding it in place.

"Tell me you love me, Alandra, as much as I love you. Tell me you'll come to Glendovia with me, marry me and be my princess. My wife."

Her lashes fluttered as she struggled to absorb everything that Nicolas was saying. His determination and declaration of love, his willingness to put her before his responsibilities to the royal family and his country.

There were so many questions spinning through her brain, but when she opened her mouth, only one thing came out.

"I love you," she murmured, her own arms lifting to curl around his shoulders and hold him as tightly as he was holding her. "It wouldn't have hurt so much to leave if I didn't."

His mouth curved in a gentle smile. "I'm very glad to hear that. Does this mean you'll be my bride?"

A thrill of happiness squeezed her heart. She wanted nothing more than to say, "Yes, yes, yes!" and cover his face with kisses. But fear had her tugging away, watching his expression to be sure everything really was okay and that she could accept his proposal without making matters in both their lives so much worse.

"What about your mother?" she asked. "I don't need to tell you how much she dislikes me, and she was horribly upset about those photographs showing up in the papers. I can't imagine she'll be very pleased to hear you've asked me to marry you."

"Whatever problems my mother has with you are her own, and she'll have to learn to live with them. *My* feelings for you are what matter, and I can tell you quite unequivocally that I adore you." The corners of his mouth curved up in a grin, and he paused a brief moment to press a kiss to her lips. "And I'll have you know that the rest of my family is equally fond of you. They supported me one hundred percent when I told them of my plans to come here and try to win you back. My father included, and you can bet that he'll do his best to bring my mother around."

"You're sure about this?" Alandra asked softly. "I don't want to do anything that could hurt you or bring trouble to your family and country."

"I couldn't be more certain," he told her, and the conviction in his tone filled her with relief. "I would give up my title for you, and if you ask it, I will. You're all that I want, and I'll do whatever it takes to have you."

She couldn't decide whether to laugh or cry as pure delight poured through her clear to her soul. "Would you take me to a hotel—one without balconies, thank you very much—and make love to me?"

His eyes glittered dangerously, his hold around her waist tightening enough to have her gasping for breath.

"A prince's job is never done," he murmured a split second before his mouth touched hers.

* * * * *

SPECIAL EDITION®

LIFE, LOVE AND FAMILY

*These contemporary romances will strike
a chord with you as heroines juggle life
and relationships on their way to true love.*

New York Times *bestselling author
Linda Lael Miller brings you
a BRAND-NEW contemporary story
featuring her fan-favorite McKettrick family.*

Meg McKettrick is surprised to be reunited with
her high school flame, Brad O'Ballivan. After
enjoying a career as a country-and-western
singer, Brad aches for a home and family…and
seeing Meg again makes him realize he still
loves her. But their pride manages to interfere
with love…until an unexpected matchmaker
gets involved.

*Turn the page for a sneak preview of
THE McKETTRICK WAY
by Linda Lael Miller
On sale November 20
wherever books are sold.*

Brad shoved the truck into gear and drove to the bottom of the hill, where the road forked. Turn left, and he'd be home in five minutes. Turn right, and he was headed for Indian Rock.

He had no damn business going to Indian Rock.

He had nothing to say to Meg McKettrick, and if he never set eyes on the woman again, it would be two weeks too soon.

He turned right.

He couldn't have said why.

He just drove straight to the Dixie Dog Drive-In.

Back in the day, he and Meg used to meet at the Dixie Dog, by tacit agreement, when either of them had been away. It had been some kind of universe thing, purely intuitive.

Passing familiar landmarks, Brad told himself he ought to turn around. The old days were gone. Things had ended badly between him and Meg anyhow, and she wasn't going to be at the Dixie Dog.

He kept driving.

He rounded a bend, and there was the Dixie Dog. Its big neon sign, a giant hot dog, was all lit up and going through its corny sequence—first it was covered in red squiggles of light, meant to suggest ketchup, and then yellow, for mustard.

Brad pulled into one of the slots next to a speaker, rolled down the truck window and ordered.

A girl roller-skated out with the order about five minutes later.

When she wheeled up to the driver's window, smiling, her eyes went wide with recognition, and she dropped the tray with a clatter.

Silently Brad swore. Damn if he hadn't forgotten he was a famous country singer.

The girl, a skinny thing wearing too much eye makeup, immediately started to cry. "I'm sorry!" she sobbed, squatting to gather up the mess.

"It's okay," Brad answered quietly, leaning to look down at her, catching a glimpse of her plastic name tag. "It's okay, Mandy. No harm done."

"I'll get you another dog and a shake right away, Mr. O'Ballivan!"

"Mandy?"

She stared up at him pitifully, sniffling. Thanks to the copious tears, most of the goop on her eyes had slid south. "Yes?"

"When you go back inside, could you not mention seeing me?"

"But you're Brad O'Ballivan!"

"Yeah," he answered, suppressing a sigh. "I know."

She rolled a little closer. "You wouldn't happen to have a picture you could autograph for me, would you?"

"Not with me," Brad answered.

"You could sign this napkin, though," Mandy said. "It's only got a little chocolate on the corner."

Brad took the paper napkin and her order pen, and scrawled his name. Handed both items back through the window.

She turned and whizzed back toward the side entrance to the Dixie Dog.

Brad waited, marveling that he hadn't considered incidents like this one before he'd decided to come back home. In retrospect, it seemed short-sighted, to say the least, but the truth was, he'd expected to be—Brad O'Ballivan.

Presently Mandy skated back out again, and this time she managed to hold on to the tray.

"I didn't tell a soul!" she whispered. "But Heather and Darlene *both* asked me why my mascara was all smeared." Efficiently she hooked the tray onto the bottom edge of the window.

Brad extended payment, but Mandy shook her head.

"The boss said it's on the house, since I dumped your first order on the ground."

He smiled. "Okay, then. Thanks."

Mandy retreated, and Brad was just reaching for the food when a bright red Blazer whipped into the space beside his. The driver's door sprang open, crashing into the metal speaker, and somebody got out in a hurry.

Something quickened inside Brad.

And in the next moment Meg McKettrick was standing practically on his running board, her blue eyes blazing.

Brad grinned. "I guess you're not over me after all," he said.

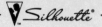

SPECIAL EDITION™

brings you a heartwarming
new McKettrick's story from

NEW YORK TIMES BESTSELLING AUTHOR

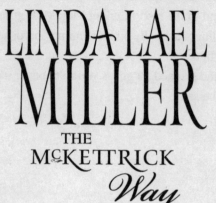

LINDA LAEL MILLER

THE McKETTRICK *Way*

Meg McKettrick is surprised to be reunited
with her high school flame, Brad O'Ballivan,
who has returned home to his family's
neighboring ranch. After seeing Meg again,
Brad realizes he still loves her. But the pride
of both manage to interfere with love...until
an unexpected matchmaker gets involved.

—— McKettrick Women ——

Available December wherever you buy books.

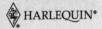

Every great love has a story to tell ™

Every Christmas gift Will and Dinah
exchange is a symbol of their love.
The tradition began on their very first
date and continues through every holiday
season—whether they're together or apart—
until tragedy strikes. And then only an
unexpected gift can make things right.

Look for

*Christmas Presents
and Past*

by
Janice Kay Johnson

Available December wherever you buy books.

Inside ROMANCE

Stay up-to-date on all your romance reading news!

Inside Romance is a FREE quarterly newsletter highlighting our upcoming series releases and promotions.

Visit
www.eHarlequin.com/InsideRomance
to sign up to receive our complimentary newsletter today!

IRN1107

Get ready to meet

THREE WISE WOMEN

with stories by

DONNA BIRDSELL, LISA CHILDS

and

SUSAN CROSBY.

Don't miss these three unforgettable stories about modern-day women and the love and new lives they find on Christmas.

Look for *Three Wise Women*
Available December wherever you buy books.

HARLEQUIN®

NeXt™

The Next Novel.com

HN88147

COMING NEXT MONTH

#1837 THE EXECUTIVE'S SURPRISE BABY—
Catherine Mann
The Garrisons
The news of his impending fatherhood was shocking…
discovering the mother of his baby didn't want to marry him—
unbelievable.

#1838 SPENCER'S FORBIDDEN PASSION—
Brenda Jackson
A Westmoreland bachelor got more than he bargained for when
he turned his hostile takeover bid into a marriage-of-convenience
offer.

#1839 RICH MAN'S VENGEFUL SEDUCTION—
Laura Wright
No Ring Required
He had one goal: seduce the woman who left him years ago and
leave her cold. Could he carry out his plan after a night together
ignites old passions?

#1840 MARRIED OR NOT?—Annette Broadrick
The last person she needed or wanted to see was her
ex-husband…until she discovered they could still be man and
wife.

#1841 HIS STYLE OF SEDUCTION—Roxanne St. Claire
She was charged with giving this millionaire a makeover. But she
was the one in for a big change...in the bedroom.

#1842 THE MAGNATE'S MARRIAGE DEMAND—
Robyn Grady
A wealthy tycoon demanded the woman pregnant with the heir
to his family dynasty marry him. But their passionate union was
anything but all business.